Three Dog Winter

Three Dog Winter

By
Elizabeth Van Steenwyk

Walker and Company
New York, New York

J
VAN

First published in the United States of America in 1987 by the Walker Publishing Company, Inc.

Library of Congress Cataloging-in-Publication Data

Van Steenwyk, Elizabeth.
Three dog winter.

Summary: The world of sled dog racing in northern Montana forms the background for a twelve-year-old boy's adjustment to his father's death, his mother's remarriage, and the integration of two families into one.
1. Sled dog racing—Fiction. 2. Remarriage—Fiction.
3. Death—Fiction. 4. Montana—Fiction. I. Title.
PZ7.V358Th   1987   [Fic]   87-10082
ISBN 0-8027-6718-4
ISBN 0-8027-6719-2 (lib. bdg.)

Printed in the United States of America

10 9 8 7 6 5 4

Text design by Laurie McBarnette

For Elizabeth, Todd, and Gretchen

Special thanks to Kay Ruch for her advice, encouragement, and expertise

Contents

Three Dog Winter

▪1▪

The First Morning

Scott heard his dog, Kaylah, the moment he awoke on the first morning in the new house. The sound confused him. He thought he was back home in Truckee and that Kaylah was calling him to hurry out for their morning run. At home it had been their special time together, while the sky still ran pink with streamers attached to the California sun at the horizon.

Now he focused on the wall nearest his bed. It wasn't papered with the little drummer boy pattern he'd awakened to practically every morning of his life, until now. This wallpaper had dull yellow flowers on it. Behind the flowers was a design the color of a pale winter sky. Great, he thought. I get to start each day looking at that weird stuff.

He rolled over and punched his pillow hard, angry with the remembering. Now it all came flooding back as Kaylah called again, a lonesome, sad sound drifting up from the barnyard to the third-floor bedroom.

I don't belong here, Kaylah seemed to be calling. I want to go home. Scott pulled the covers over his head, burrowed deep, away from the sound, away from the hurt the sound brought back. He pictured Kaylah sitting outside, his white muzzle turned upward, his mouth a perfect O as he bayed his sadness.

Poor Kaylah, Scott thought. He's only a dog. How can I explain to him what happened? How can I tell him that Mom lost her head over some guy named David Hartfield and married him, just like that, only eight months after Dad died? How can I tell Kaylah I feel the same way he does about leaving home and moving to Montana, to the middle of nowhere?

Scott sat up abruptly. How could Mom forget so fast? How could she marry again, and so soon? Sure, she was lonesome after Dad died. And seeing Mr. Hartfield at her high-school reunion was probably fun, but she didn't have to marry him.

Kaylah bayed again, longer and louder this time, and Scott knew he had to do something fast. If Kaylah woke Mom and Mr. Hartfield, they could get angry enough to make him give his dog away. In fact, Mom had hinted before they moved that Kaylah would be better off staying behind with friends in Truckee. But no way could Scott let that happen. Not unless he stayed, too.

Holy mackerel! Now Scott remembered something else. Last night he'd tied Kaylah in the barn so he wouldn't try to go home. Now he was outside, sitting by the back door.

Scott jumped out of bed and padded across the bare floor. Jeez, it was cold up here. Only the middle of October and he was freezing already. At least there was one good thing about it. The snow might come sooner and last longer. Somehow, some way, he would race again.

He raised the window and leaned out, looking over the pitched roof of the porch below.

"Kaylah," he called in a hoarse whisper. "Cool it, boy. I'll be down in a sec." Scott dressed quickly in jeans and a flannel shirt. But where were his socks? Had he already put them away in the dresser? Yes, there they were, his favorites with the blue band around the cuffs.

As he pulled them from the drawer, he glanced up and saw his reflection in the mirror. He still looked the same; that much hadn't changed in his life, anyway. Everyone said he looked like Dad and he couldn't argue that. The same chunk of wheat-colored hair flopped over his eyes. Mom called their color Scottish blue. And his frame was like Dad's, beanpole tall and skinny, though no muscles yet to speak of. He'd better start lifting weights and beef up because he'd need more strength for what he wanted to do.

He slipped on his socks and carried his shoes as he hurried down two flights of stairs, hoping he'd meet no one, especially Brad Hartfield. Why did Mr. Hartfield have to have kids anyway? Particularly a real winner like Brad? Scott didn't want to explain to anyone, but especially not to Brad, that he needed to comfort a homesick dog and that maybe in the comforting he'd feel comforted, too.

As he stepped outside and stood on the back porch, Scott breathed in the icy air, then quickly put on his shoes. Before he could get them tied, he was nearly knocked over by Kaylah's powerful body hurled against him in a frenzy of wagging, licking, and barking.

"Hey," Scott said, laughing. "Stop it, will you?" He sat on the porch steps and tied his shoes while Kaylah nudged and nuzzled him. Then he threw his arms around the dog's neck and burrowed his face in the soft, thick ruff. Scott smelled his earthiness and knew he must have spent some of the night in the barn with the other animals before he broke the rope to come outside.

Now Scott glanced up and saw the Hartfield's farm dog come around the corner of the barn. He stopped when he saw Scott and Kaylah.

"Kaylah," Scott whispered, looking into the dog's dark, almond-shaped eyes. "We're too old for this mushy stuff. Besides, look who's watching. It's that dumb Bruno. Bruno and Brad, what a combo." Scott untied the frayed rope from Kaylah's collar and smoothed the silvery ruff around it.

Now Bruno sat down and began to scratch. He must be part retriever, Scott thought, taking in the long, wavy fur and plumed tail. Maybe his mom was a Golden, and his father a traveling man.

"Come on, let's see where you stayed last night, Kaylah." Scott jumped up and Kaylah padded down the steps after him. They crossed the barnyard quickly, Scott's shoes crunching on the gravel surface.

Just before stepping inside the barn, Scott glanced back at the house. Was that someone watching from a second-floor window? Maybe his sister, Caroline, was awake, too, bothered by the strangeness of this still, flat land.

No, not Caroline. Caroline wouldn't be bothered. She'd been having a great time since they arrived yesterday afternoon. And last night at supper, she was so giggly with Mr. Hartfield that Scott had been ready to throw up. Give her food to fill her roly-poly eight-year-old body and she'd be a happy traitor anywhere. She didn't miss Dad, not for a minute.

"Come on," Scott whispered. His hand automatically searched for the light switch on the right-hand side of the door and flipped it on. Instantly the barn was flooded with brightness, and he had to blink several times as he followed

Kaylah inside. A lone milk cow in her stall glanced up at them as she chewed on her cud.

Scott followed Kaylah down the aisle, while two quarter horses stirred uneasily in their stalls on the left. Across from them an Appaloosa put her nose over the stall gate. Scott stopped to scratch the warm muzzle. "Here's a friendly face," he said to Kaylah, but the dog had moved out of sight into an empty stall at the far end of the barn.

Scott knew that's where he'd been headed, knew that's where the dog intuitively would go. He hurried down the aisle now and stepped into the stall. Kaylah stood beside the sled, waiting.

For a second, the eager look on the dog's face nearly broke Scott's control, his promise to himself that he'd never cry again. Twelve-year-olds don't cry. How many times had he told himself this before he finally buried the tears somewhere back in Truckee, back with Dad?

He shook his mind free, forced it to move to something else. Looking at the sled more closely, he tried to give it a close inspection as Dad would have done. He sighed. It hadn't fared too well in the move from California.

What did he need to do first? He was grateful that the runners looked okay because he'd never be able to repair them. He'd never have the patience to bolt ash board pieces less than two inches wide over runners of plastic. The broken basket slats presented no problem because they could be mended with some epoxy and clamped together until the glue dried. What luck that the warped-wood brushbow hadn't been damaged. It still was poised in its upswept arc, curved higher to take deep snow with ease. Sleds are truly beautiful, Scott thought.

After these few repairs the sled would look nearly the way it had when Dad built it. It was a thirty-five-pound racing model, almost eight feet long, but built higher and slightly wider to suit Dad's frame.

He had lashed each joint with tough nylon, mortising wood to wood first, leaving some joints loose so the sled could give way gracefully over bumps, while others were bound tightly to permit a twisting action around curves.

Scott remembered that the sled turned and tracked with a grace that took his breath away as he watched. It was a champion's sled, he thought, and it will be again.

"We'll race again, wait and see, Kaylah." He ruffled the dog's thick black-and-white coat. "But you have to be patient. You have to learn to wait. For starters, I've got to fix the sled and put in some jog time with you. And the biggest wait of all is for snow. But it's going to be different anyway, with or without the wait. You don't have a team to lead now. It's just you and me."

Kaylah looked up alertly, past Scott, to the stall opening. Then his tail began to wag as Bruno trotted in. Bruno wandered over to the sled, nosed it, then lifted his leg on a runner.

"No, you don't," Scott yelled. "This is Kaylah's, you can't mark it for your own."

Scott patted Bruno's head a moment, then let him roll in the straw on the floor. Bruno was nearly the same size as Kaylah, but not as deep-chested nor as full-muscled across the shoulders. Dad used to say that any dog could pull a sled if he had the desire for it, so maybe Bruno could be on somebody's team.

But not mine, Scott thought. In the first place he's Brad's

dog, and in the second, he'd not a Mally. I want a matched team, all Malamutes, like the ones that Dad used to drive. None of this patched-up stuff for me.

Scott picked at loose pieces of wood on the sled, remembering. One by one the dogs had been sold during the months of Dad's illness. It cost too much to feed them, Mom had said. And there was no one to work them, even when Scott insisted he was big enough. And old enough.

But Scott had to admit, even to himself, that fourteen powerful Malamutes on two teams had been a lot of dog power even for a man like Dad when he had been strong and well. Besides, Scott knew they had needed the money from the sale of the dogs, especially after Mom quit her photography job on the newspaper to stay home and take care of Dad.

But Dad had insisted that Scott be allowed to keep Kaylah, the best lead dog, and Mom promised. Now Kaylah and the sled were all that were left of Dad's dream of winning. Unless . . . unless . . . Scott made them come true. And he would. He definitely would.

Kaylah and Bruno turned suddenly to the stall opening, ears alert. Scott turned with them. "What did you hear?" he asked them.

Brad stepped into the stall as if he'd been standing just around the corner for some time. His dark hair and eyes were younger versions of his dad's.

"Do you always talk to your dog like that?" Brad's hands were deep in his back pockets, his feet planted far apart as if he dared Scott to answer him.

"Don't you ever talk to yours?" Scott tried to sound friendly, but he didn't feel it. He'd known this guy less than twenty-four hours, and already he could feel the hostility between them.

Brad shrugged, stepped closer, and appeared to examine the sled. "Think you'll ever get that thing in shape again? It looks pretty beat up to me."

Kaylah bounded over to Brad and waited to be introduced, but Brad jumped back, nearly tripping over his own feet.

"It's okay, he's friendly. Mallys are friendly dogs. They're just so big, sometimes they scare people."

"Who says I'm scared?" Brad's dark eyes gave off sparks. "Dad says you can't trust strange dogs. One almost bit my brother once."

"This dog's not strange," Scott said. "I've known him since he was born."

Brad put out a cautious hand, and Kaylah nudged it with his nose. Scott nearly laughed, sensing that Kaylah was coaxing, teasing Brad, wanting to play. Bruno watched and waited for an invitation to join in.

"What time does the school bus come tomorrow?" Scott asked, trying to think of things to say.

"A quarter to seven."

"How come the bus leaves so early?" Scott felt irritated, having to coax every little bit of information out of Brad, word by word.

"Told you last night, we're ten miles from Box Elder and the school we go to."

That's right, Scott thought. We went through this last night at the supper table, with Mom as the referee. How old are you? I'm twelve. How old are you? I'm twelve, too. Same age, same grade, wouldn't you know.

Caroline had it better. She was two years younger than

Howdy, Brad's brother. Even though all of them would be in the same elementary school, Caroline would be in third grade while Howdy was in fifth. Different rooms at least.

Scott looked down and scuffed his feet in the straw on the floor. "I need to fix up a bed for Kaylah since he aims to sleep in here. Should have done it last night, but there was so much going on." He spoke more to himself than to Brad.

They hadn't brought much from Truckee. At least it didn't seem like much at the time, but still they managed to fill a good-sized do-it-yourself moving van. By the time his furniture was hauled to the third-floor bedroom and the rest of the stuff unpacked, it had been time for supper.

"Does your dad always do the cooking?" Scott asked suddenly.

"Who else is there?" Brad said. His tone was sharp, and Scott wished he hadn't asked. Mom had told him and Caroline about the first Mrs. Hartfield and how she had simply walked out a few years ago.

"My mom cooks really neat," Scott said. "You'll really like her cooking."

"Doesn't matter much," Brad said. "I'm not gonna be here much longer. As soon as I hear from my mom, I'm moving to Billings."

Scott shrugged, wondering if Mr. Hartfield knew about this plan, whatever it was. Personally he didn't care where Brad lived. "I have to find Kaylah's dishes and kibble," he said.

Scott left the barn and headed for the house, Kaylah trotting by his side. There was a light burning in an upstairs bedroom now, and Scott guessed that to be Mom's room—rather, *their* room. Last night, on his way up to the third floor, Scott had seen Mr. Hartfield carry Mom over the threshhold into the room. His stomach still churned at the thought of Mom lying beside some other man who wasn't Dad. It just wasn't right. He kicked at a pebble and sent it flying.

Suddenly a wave of longing for the world he'd left behind in Truckee washed over him. Naturally he missed Jamie the most. Good old Jamie, his best buddy, had practically lived at their house. Morning, noon, and night he was there, learning sled racing from Dad, too.

Scott shook himself free of his memories. Why did happy times hurt so much in their remembering?

"Wait here, Kaylah," he said at the back door. "I think your stuff is in the pantry."

Mr. Hartfield turned from the sink as Scott opened the door. "Morning, Scott." His booming voice took over the entire kitchen. "You're up early."

"Kaylah was making a fuss, so I thought I'd better settle him down."

"I heard him. What's his trouble?" Mr. Hartfield began measuring coffee into a pot.

"He wants to go home."

Mr. Hartfield turned to look at him, a spoonful of coffee poised in mid-air. "He is home, Scott. Guess it will take him a day or two to adjust."

"Maybe." Scott glanced at the table set for six people. Three and three make six, but that's all it makes, he thought.

"I have to get Kaylah's food." Scott looked around for the pantry. Which door was it? This house was so big and there were so many rooms and floors, he'd never learn where everything was. Suddenly he felt hot, sort of trapped, and the air wasn't getting to his lungs. I have to get out of here, have to get . . .

Mr. Hartfield was standing in front of him now. "Scott, it's going to take time for all of us to adjust. It will be a lot easier if we all try to be friends right away. How about it?"

His hand was outstretched before Scott, waiting for him to shake it. Scott looked at that powerful hand, the calluses worn to white toughness from the heavy work of running a wheat farm.

Oh, shoot, might as well, Scott thought. The back door opened and slammed as they shook hands. Scott looked over his shoulder to see Brad staring at him. He saw the warning in Brad's eyes and quickly pulled away from Mr. Hartfield's grasp.

"That dumb dog of yours bit me." Brad spit the words out at Scott as if they were fruit pits.

"No, he didn't. I was there—" Scott began.

"Not in the barn. Just now, he grabbed my hand."

"Let me see, Brad." Mr. Hartfield was at Brad's side in two strides, looking. "I don't know . . ."

"Kaylah doesn't bite," Scott said. "He's never bitten anyone in his life, never even tried, never wanted to."

"Then what do you call that?" Brad yelled, uncontrolled anger in his voice as he shoved his hand at Scott.

Scott stared at the red marks on the heel of Brad's left hand. The marks could be anything at all, scratches from a nail, anything.

"I say you made a mistake," Scott said.

"Are you calling me a liar?" Brad's voice was as friendly as a snake's hiss.

"That's what I'm doing." Scott watched him, wanting to punch his face out.

"Boys, ease off," Mr. Hartfield warned. "This isn't a fight."

But it was, and Brad had won the first round. Even

though Scott knew Kaylah would never bite under normal circumstances, being in a strange place, surrounded by strangers wasn't normal. And Brad had won, no two ways about it. He's planted a seed of doubt in everybody's mind about the dog. Even Scott's.

·2·

An Alarming Discovery

Scott led Kaylah back to the barn, to the stall where the sled was. Somehow that small square of space seemed safer than any other spot on this huge farm.

"Come on, Kaylah. I'll feed you in your own pad and then we'll talk about you biting that guy." It worried Scott. He knew, just knew, that Kaylah would never bite, but something had happened.

Inside the stall Scott poured kibble into Kaylah's blue bowl, then mixed it with some canned food left over from last night. He put it on the floor, and the dog began to gulp it down.

"You're gonna get a giant-sized bellyache, eating like that," Scott said, leaning against a wall.

Kaylah looked up, a small bit of meat still stuck to his nose, and he burped before checking his bowl once again. Then he lay down near Scott's feet and rolled in the straw on the floor.

"Maybe, if we stay here long enough, the whole scene inside will blow over," Scott said, scratching Kaylah's rump with the toe of his boot.

But he had to face it. He was worried sick about Brad's accusation. What would happen to Kaylah if it were true, or even if Mom and Mr. Hartfield believed it? Mom wouldn't believe it. She'd be on his side. She knew Mallys as well as he did. He couldn't lose Kaylah . . .

Suddenly Scott ran to the sled. Putting one foot on a runner, he grabbed the handlebar and began to pump with the other leg as if he were on a scooter. He bent low, squinted through imaginary snow pelting his face, and shouted, "Go, dogs, go!"

Kaylah leaped to his feet, barking, and then jumped at Scott. "Down, boy, down," he yelled. "I didn't mean it."

Scott and Kaylah fell to the floor in a tangle of arms and legs, playing a wild game that was Kaylah's favorite. They rolled and tugged until Scott grabbed the dog's collar to signal the end of it. Kaylah looked at him, eyes shining, waiting, wanting more.

"That's enough, you nasty, vicious critter," Scott said, fending off the excited dog while he tried to spit straw from his mouth.

I've got to remember, Scott thought. I've got to remember what Dad said about giving commands without meaning them. Mallys know and remember. They're so crazy to run that their remembered commands send them into orbit.

Kaylah turned suddenly to the stall's opening. Scott turned too, to see Howdy peeking around the corner of the opening. He looked scared and suspicious.

"Is he really vicious?" Howdy asked. "I just heard Brad saying . . ."

"No." Scott came down on the word hard. "He's a good dog. He's okay."

"Then why did Brad—"

"It's a mistake, Howdy. Come on, pet him."

Howdy loosened his hold on the stall gate and took a step inside. "I don't know . . ."

Scott walked over to Howdy, noticing how he towered over the kid. Howdy was such a skinny pipsqueak for being ten years old. He was little all over except for his head, which seemed as if it belonged to someone else about two sizes bigger.

Scott took him by the hand and led him to the dog. They knelt down before Kaylah. "Just pet him nice and easy. Doesn't he have soft fur?"

"Yeah. Just like Bruno's, only thicker." Kaylah gave Howdy's nose a slobbery lick.

Howdy giggled and wiped. "Guess he likes me," he said. "I must taste good."

This kid is pretty decent, Scott thought. Better than his brother anyway.

"Oh, I almost forget," Howdy said, standing up. "Your mom sent me to get you."

Scott sighed. The sound had ragged edges to it. "Okay. Guess I better see what she wants." But he knew all right.

They headed for the house, Howdy walking close to Scott, now and then reaching out a hand to Kaylah. A thought began to buzz around Scott's brain, like a gnat refusing to light. Suddenly he caught it. What if Brad had said something to Kaylah just before coming inside? Maybe he had said a word that sounded like a command, and the dog had started jumping around, doing his crazy routine. Any word might have done it, like "Go away" or just "Go." Then Kaylah could have made those marks on Brad's hands. He wasn't biting, just playing.

It wasn't much to go on, but it was something. He'd explain it to Mom and Mr. Hartfield before they gave him a lecture or made him get rid of the dog. He felt better now as he stood by the porch steps.

"Stay right here, Kaylah," he said as he went inside.

Mom was pouring juice from a pitcher and looked up as Scott entered. She wore a fancy new bathrobe with ruffly things at her throat. Scott wondered what had become of the old blue one that left fuzz all over his face when she hugged him? He couldn't remember a time when she hadn't worn the blue one. Like the times he'd been sick in the middle of the night when he was little. Things sure were different now, and getting more different all the time.

"Morning, Scott," Mom said. "How did you sleep?"

"Okay, except I heard Kaylah and got up to see what was bothering him." Mom's eyes seemed a lot bluer this morning, and she was wearing lipstick. Lipstick at breakfast, for crumb's sake. That's a first.

"I heard him, too. Is he all right now?"

"Yeah. I just fed him." Scott waited, waited for something to happen, for someone to say something. Mr. Hartfield was flipping pancakes on a griddle at the stove. Brad was just sitting at the table, playing with a fork, tapping it over and over on his plate.

Finally Mr. Hartfield turned, carrying a tower of pancakes on a platter. "Sit down, Scott. Hope you like my pancakes. We always have them on Sunday mornings."

"Better wash your hands, Howdy," Mom said quietly. Howdy looked at his dad, who nodded. "You too, Scott," Mom said.

They walked to the sink together. "We never had to wash our hands before," Howdy whispered.

"Get used to it," Scott said, grabbing a towel. "You'll be

doing lots of it." Jamie used to complain about it too, he thought.

Scott went back to the table and sat down at a place near Mom. Mr. Hartfield looked at him. "We've decided, your mom and I," he said, "that whatever happened with Kaylah out there was an accident. Isn't that right, Brad?"

"Yeah." But Brad didn't believe it, Scott thought. Not for a minute.

"Kaylah's shots are up to date," Scott said. "And he didn't mean it, if he did it . . ."

"He did it." Brad said it so quietly that Scott wondered if he'd really spoken.

"That's enough," Mr. Hartfield said. "We're going to make sure that Brad's hand doesn't get an infection, and then forget that this happened. Got that?"

Scott breathed in a great gulp of air and nearly choked on his orange juice.

"After breakfast Brad and Howdy need to show Scott around." Mr. Hartfield kept the platters of pancakes and eggs and bacon moving. "He needs to know where the bus stop is, for one thing."

"Okay." Howdy stuffed his mouth with food. "I'll show him my secret way."

"Secret," Brad snorted. "It's so secret that even the dumb sheep can follow it."

"Where's Caroline?" Scott looked at Mom. "It wasn't like his sister to miss a meal.

"I checked on her just before I came downstairs," Mom said. "She was sleeping so hard I decided not to wake her up."

"Listen everyone, I have something to tell you." Mr.

Hartfield smiled at them all now, but especially at Mom, who smiled back. Mr. Hartfield's eyes looked drippy, as if they were ready to melt. Scott sighed, wondering how long all this lovey-dovey stuff would go on.

"What, Dad?" Howdy helped himself to another stack of pancakes. "What's going to happen?"

"Your mom is going to start doing all the cooking."

"My mom?" Howdy said. "Is she coming back?"

"Man, you are so dumb," Brad said. "You are really dumb."

"I'm not either dumb." Howdy's face clouded over.

"Brad." Mr. Hartfield tried to control his voice. "It was my fault. I didn't say it right. Howdy is not dumb."

"What your father means is that, starting tomorrow morning, I'm going to do the cooking," Mom said quietly.

"And I can't wait." More smiles from Mr. Hartfield. "Of course, I still get to make the pancakes on Sunday mornings. Right, boys?"

Brad and Howdy looked at one another and shrugged. Finally Howdy said, "Right." Then he looked at Mom. "Do you know how to make fried chicken and spaghetti?"

"We'll start with fried chicken tomorrow night," Mom said. "How about you, Brad? Do you have any favorites?"

"No." He made the word the shortest it had ever been.

"Well, then, I'll just surprise you." Mom's face turned kind of pink, to match her bathrobe.

"As long as we're talking about surprises, I've got one for everybody, but especially Scott." Mr. Hartfield stood up and began to clear the table.

Brad stood up, too, and headed for the back door.

"Where're you going, Brad? Don't you want to hear about my surprise?"

"I'm too big for surprises." He grabbed his jacket from a peg by the door and went outside.

"Anyway"—Mr. Hartfield's voice sounded too loud in the sudden silence—"I read in the paper about some sled-dog workouts that are going to be held near Havre next weekend."

Scott felt a rush of excitement. Workouts. That meant there was a sled-dog club, probably more than one, conducting practice runs, getting ready for good snow. Some people even had dogs and equipment for sale at workouts. Maybe . . .

"What do you say, Scott?" Mr. Hartfield asked. "Are you interested? I think it would be great if we all went. I've always wondered about sled dogs, how you get 'em to run and all that. Maybe we could put a Hartfield team together." He kept on talking, kind of babbling, trying to fill up the quiet in the kitchen with his words.

Hartfield team? Scott thought. I'm only interested in a McClure team. Why can't he figure that out?

"Scott, what do you say?" Mom sounded a little testy. "I think it's a great idea. We'll all go, and I'll fix a picnic, just like I used to. I'll bring lots of hot chocolate in case it turns really cold."

"Oh, boy," Howdy said. "I'll go if we're going to have a picnic."

"Then it's all settled," Mr. Hartfield said. "Howdy, if you're finished eating, why don't you take Scott outside now and show him where the bus stop is."

"Okay." Howdy grabbed the last piece of bacon before he slipped out of his chair, wiping his greasy fingers on his jeans.

They went outdoors and Howdy led the way around the

corner of the house, turning in a direction away from the barn. There was a lawn here, bare and brown now, sloping down to a circular drive. A quick, biting wind scattered brittle leaves ahead of them as they walked along the driveway.

"Where are we going?" Scott asked, turning up his jacket collar.

Howdy pointed a skinny finger. "See those trees over there?"

Scott looked across a field of broken, brown cornstalks to a clump of cottonwoods. "Yeah, I see 'em."

"We're headed for my secret path right through them."

Brad had caught up now. "You and your secrets," he said. "Everybody knows about that path through the woods."

"Not everybody." Howdy's eyes blinked fast enough to send coded signals. "Lots of people don't."

Brad and Howdy continued to pick away at one another as Scott gradually tuned them out. He had better things to think about, like the workouts next Saturday. But how could he keep Mr. Hartfield from interfering? Maybe he could talk to Mom before they went, explain how he wanted . . . needed . . . to do this by himself.

Scott felt Kaylah's nose touch his hand in greeting before the Mally ran ahead to explore the woods.

"Better keep that dog on a leash when he leaves our place," Brad said. "The guy who owns the spread next to ours shoots anything that strays onto his property."

"Some neighbor," Scott said. He whistled for Kaylah, expecting him to return quickly, the way he'd been trained by Dad. But Kaylah ignored Scott and ranged farther ahead.

"Minds real nice," Brad said under his breath.

Scott felt a bubble of anger swill around inside him. So when did he get to be such an expert? Bruno wasn't exactly a candidate for dog of the year.

"Maybe we'd better get him," Howdy said. He entered the woods first and headed toward a path that zigzagged through the trees.

"Kaylah," Scott called again. Where did he go? He never wandered off, not without a reason. Let's see now, how would he handle it? Sled dogs had to respond fast when they were on the trail. If they didn't, there was no telling what might happen. An accident, a fight, losing the trail and getting lost . . . he hated to think about it.

Scott saw a flash of black and white flit through the trees. There he was. "Come here, Kaylah. Come here, boy." Scott ran across the uneven ground covered with brush. Finally he spotted the dog again, nosing around in a pile of leaves.

I wonder what he's found, Scott thought. Something dead and about nine days old probably. Maybe an old rat. Ick. "Come," he called. He had to make the dog obey now and keep the discipline consistent, otherwise he'd lose control. Dad always said that.

Kaylah continued to ignore him. "Doggone you," Scott said. He picked up a dirt clod and heaved it toward the Mally. Did something stir in the leaves? Maybe the rat wasn't dead yet.

He decided to take a quick look and ran forward to stare down. Oh, god. Oh, my god. It was a dog. Thin, ragged, suffering, needing help. The aching in the dog's eyes hurt Scott so much that, for a second, he had to turn away from it. He could feel the dog's pain inside his own body. But he had to look again. He couldn't stand not to look again.

Scott forced himself to look for bleeding or oozing or a gash, whatever had injured the dog. There it was, blood all over its leg, matted, dried, rusty brown, nearly matching his coat. The dog had been shot, probably. Sure, that guy on the next spread. Shot and left to die.

"Scott, where are you?" Caroline's voice came from somewhere back on the path, but there was no time to answer. Besides, she'd bawl and maybe scare the dog and he didn't need that.

"Scott, hey Scott." Howdy now, closer than Caroline. They were coming, but he couldn't wait. He had to hurry, do something.

He slipped off his jacket and covered the dog. "I'll be right back," he whispered. "Don't die. Please don't die."

Scott ran toward the house, feeling something wet on his cheeks. For a second he thought it was snowing. Another second later, he had to admit to himself that he was crying.

▪3▪

So Much To Worry About

Scott ran back to the house, feeling hot and cold, scared and dizzy. His breakfast lurched around in his stomach. Colored spots danced in front of his eyes. His breath felt all bunched up in his throat. No more dying, he thought. No more dying around me.

"Scott," he heard someone yell. The sound came from behind him, yet it didn't connect. It didn't seem to have anything to do with him. "Hey, Scott . . . " But the rest of the words drifted away like smoke as he ran.

Finally, finally, he neared the house and barn. Where would they be? Inside? Outside? Try inside first! Doing dishes together. Lovey-dovey dishes.

Bruno ran around the corner of the house and danced his greeting, nearly tripping Scott. "Beat it," Scott yelled. "Git." He clattered up the back porch steps, taking them two at a time, and charged into the kitchen.

Mom and Mr. Hartfield stood near the sink, their arms around each other. Scott knew they'd been kissing. They had that look. But right now he didn't care what he'd interrupted.

"Dog," Scott managed to gasp, and pointed toward the woods. "Hurt. Hurt bad."

"Not Bruno," Mr. Hartfield said, looking at the dog on the back porch.

"Kaylah?" Mom's voice sounded suddenly choked and full.

"Strange dog." Scott pulled in a long deep breath. "Brad said your neighbor . . . "

Mr. Hartfield brought his fist down hard on the counter. "Damn him." Then he was in motion. "I'll get some things from the barn and follow you."

"I'll get dressed." Mom ran from the room.

Then Scott was running back to the woods, Bruno at his heels. He saw Brad and Howdy running toward him.

"Scott," Howdy began. "You're acting so weird."

"Did you see a ghost?" Brad asked, smirking.

Scott didn't break his stride, didn't bother to waste effort on words. He kept running until he was back in the woods, crashing around trees, stumbling over fallen branches and broken tree roots.

Which way? Which way? "Kaylah," he called. Why couldn't he see Kaylah? Why didn't he bark?

Bruno ranged ahead, sensing the need for it, his nose to the ground. "Easy," Scott said. "Don't scare anybody."

Then Scott saw Kaylah, nose down, tail up, standing guard and waiting. Scott ran over, pushed him aside and knelt beside the injured dog.

"Don't die," he whispered. "Everything's going to be okay."

Mr. Hartfield came, and a minute later, Mom and Caroline. Everyone began to talk and ask questions at the same time, until Caroline burst into tears and Brad told her to shut up. Then Caroline cried louder, and Mom led her away. All the while Mr. Hartfield was bent over the dog, finally wrapping him in a tattered horse blanket and carrying him back to the barn.

"Is he still alive?" Scott asked as they went inside. But no one answered. No one knew.

"Put him in here, Dad," Howdy yelled, running toward the stall with the sled in it.

Mr. Hartfield put the dog down gently, on the straw-covered floor and looked up at them. "Brad, call Doc Hansen," he said.

"He's a horse doctor."

"He's a vet. Now go on."

Brad left as Mom came in. "I'm heating water and I've brought some rags," she said. "I don't know what else to do."

"That's a start," Mr. Hartfield said.

Mom and Mr. Hartfield worked over the dog while they waited for the vet. No sound came from the animal, no movement, nothing. Just a bag of bones, lying there, hurting.

Finally Doc Hansen came and shooed the kids and Kaylah and Bruno out of the stall. Mom and Mr. Hartfield stayed with him, and their voices rose and fell in quiet waves of words.

A long time later, Doc came out. "That's a strong dog in there," he said. His thin gray hair stood up, like wires, around his head. "He was shot in the leg, but it was a clean shot. No bones broken, but a lot of blood lost, so it's going to be touch and go for awhile. Let's hope the antibiotics do the job, although some TLC will help. Think you can handle that?" Small wrinkles creased his face when he cracked a tired smile.

Mr. Hartfield came out of the stall. "We'll all help," he

said. "Meantime, spread the word around, Doc. If anybody's missing a nearly grown rust-colored setter, this is probably him."

"I've got an idea," Mom said. "I'll take his picture and maybe the newspaper in town will publish it. We ought to find his owner that way."

Scott sighed a long, ragged sigh that scraped his insides. What if it had been Kaylah? He bent down and hugged him fiercely, burying his face in the deep ruff of fur around the dog's throat. Tomorrow he'd lock Kaylah in the barn before he went to school so he wouldn't follow along to the bus stop, through those terrible woods. He wouldn't take chances with Kaylah.

Scott smelled bacon frying the next morning as he hurried to the second-floor landing. And there was the smell of cinnamon too. That's right, Mom was taking over the cooking today. She was starting off with her world-famous cinnamon rolls. That's what Dad used to call them.

"What are you smiling at?" Caroline stood in the doorway of her room, looking sleepy and suspicious at the same time. Her dark red hair looked hopelessly tangled and her dress was buttoned all wrong.

"You, dopey," Scott said. "Better hurry up. The school bus comes in twenty minutes and that doesn't leave much time, especially if you want to see how the dog is." Already Scott had begun to think of him as Rusty.

"I almost forgot about the dog," Caroline said. "I'll hurry real fast."

Mom turned from the stove, and Mr. Hartfield looked up from the table when Scott walked into the kitchen.

"Morning," Scott said.

"Morning, Scott." Mr. Hartfield pointed to a chair at the

table. "Sit down, have some breakfast. These rolls are the greatest."

"They're world-famous," Scott said, glancing at Mom. He began to button his jacket.

She flicked him a look of remembering before she asked, "Where are you going? You can't go to school without breakfast."

"I want to see how the dog is," Scott said, "and lock Kaylah in the barn so he won't follow me to the bus. Will you let him out later this morning?"

"Sure," Mom said. "Here, take a roll with you. They're nice and hot."

Mom was right. The roll was warm and tasted the way he knew it would. He stood on the back porch and turned up his jacket collar, looking for Kaylah.

Oh, no. What if he's gone back to the woods? For a moment Scott's feelings burned his throat. He swallowed crumbs of the roll and felt as if he would choke on their hugeness. They seemed to take forever going down.

Then Kaylah appeared in the doorway of the barn, waiting for him.

"There you are," Scott said, running across the barnyard. "You've been playing nurse."

He ran inside the stall and knelt beside Rusty. "Morning. I think Mom's got plans for your breakfast later on." He had smelled rich beef broth simmering in the kitchen. Mom always gave it to their sick or pregnant dogs at home in Truckee.

Rusty blinked several times at him. This morning his deep amber eyes had lost their glazed look.

"I'll be back later and tell you all about my first day of school here in the wilds of Montana." Now Kaylah returned and sat down in the straw near Rusty. "Take good care of him, Kaylah." Scott shut the stall gate firmly before he left.

Scott thought about Kaylah and Rusty during the long bus ride into Box Elder, and he thought about the new school waiting for him. Kaylah seemed to be forming an instant attachment to Rusty; perhaps he missed the companionship of his old team. So why didn't he show an interest in Bruno? Maybe because the farm was Bruno's territory, his turf, and Kaylah knew he was an outsider, like Rusty. Like me, Scott thought. Me, too.

Don't get too close, Scott wanted to say to Kaylah. It hurts too much when you get close to someone and lose him.

Scott had Phys. Ed. during first recess, the same time as Brad. Fortunately they weren't picked for the same kickball team, so Scott didn't have to talk to him. Scott hadn't really talked to anyone yet, just sort of drifted along, wishing the day would end. Suddenly he missed Jamie with an intensity he could feel.

Kickball is dumb, he thought. So are most sports in school. Why don't they teach something exciting like sled-dog racing? For a moment Scott pictured himself coming to the teacher's rescue. The teacher hadn't had any experience so he called on Scott, and Scott showed the guys how to handle a sled, how to harness the team, and how to win. Oh, yeah. On the big day . . .

"Hey, watch it."

The ball hit him squarely on the head.

"Great catch," Brad said, retrieving the ball and throwing it to a teammate.

Scott tried to concentrate, but it was hard when his brain

wanted to be a million miles away. Ten miles at least, back at the farm with Kaylah and Rusty.

At lunchtime Scott walked into the cafeteria and hesitated. Some of the sixth-grade boys had dibs on a table to themselves, with Brad seated at the end as if he was president or something. He looked up and saw Scott, but made no motion for him to come over.

So I won't, Scott thought. No way will I go over there.

He filled his tray and turned around, bumping into a girl who looked sort of familiar.

"Sorry," he said. "Didn't mean to plow into you like that."

"No problem," she said. "You're Brad Hartfield's new brother, aren't you?"

"Yeah, I guess." Crumb, what a handle.

"I'm Michelle Weaver," she said. "We're in the same room in case you hadn't noticed."

She wasn't exactly a girl who'd get your attention, Scott thought, looking at her. Kind of washed out and a little on the bony side. Her jeans looked as if they were being worn by sticks.

"You want to eat with me?" she asked. "Or do you plan to eat right there in the middle of the aisle?"

Scott looked around. The tables were filling up quickly and there seemed to be no place else to go. And she was right. He couldn't stand here, like the nerd of the week, especially since he knew Brad was watching.

"Why not?" Scott shrugged. "Lead the way."

She wound her way among the tables, past the strange faces who turned to look up at him, mouths open, lunch exposed. Finally she arrived at a corner table, with only two kids seated there.

"This is where I always sit," she said. She began to unload her tray.

He chose a seat across from her and removed the plate of tuna casserole and a dish of pale-colored jello from his tray. Before he sat down, a couple more kids arrived. Finally the table was filled and everyone began to eat, now and then glancing at him.

"This is Brad Hartfield's new brother," Michelle said after a while. "His name's Scott something."

"McClure. Scott McClure." Next thing he knew they'd be calling him Scott Hartfield and he wouldn't have that. Not even once.

"You're from California," a younger-looking version of Michelle said. "I heard at recess."

"Right."

"That's my sister, Barbie," Michelle said. Then she put names with the other faces at the table.

"So where's your surfboard?" Robert asked. He laughed in a shrieking pitch that could be heard all over the cafeteria. Scott glanced around, feeling his face heat up, and saw Brad and his group staring.

"What are those Hollywood chicks really like?" Jeffrey asked.

Scott jabbed at his dish of jello. "There's a lot more to California than surfing and the movies."

"What's the matter, can't you take a little kidding?" Robert asked. He wound up to shriek again, but Scott choked it off with a glowering look.

"What did you do down there in California?" Michelle asked.

"I raced sled dogs with my dad."

"No kidding?" Barbie asked. "You mean you had enough snow?"

"There's more snow in some parts of California than some parts of Montana."

"Did you bring your dogs with you?" Michelle leaned forward. Her pale blue eyes suddenly sparkled.

"I brought one, but I need more," Scott said. "I need three. As soon as I have them, I'll start their training, then enter races."

"Sounds neat," Michelle said. "Maybe we can watch you sometime."

"Sure," Scott shrugged. "Any time."

"You really mean it?" Michelle asked.

Scott began to feel a little uneasy. Why was she getting so worked up? "Anybody can come to the races."

Then everyone looked up and so did Scott, to find Brad standing beside him.

"Nice going, Scott," he whispered. "You sure know how to pick 'em." He turned and walked away with a couple of guys, their snickers lingering behind them.

What was Brad talking about? Scott couldn't figure it. Pick what? Pick who? He looked at the faces of the kids at the table. They were all looking at him, patiently waiting for him to go on with his talk of sled dogs.

Suddenly Scott understood. He was news. Somebody from somewhere else. He'd also invited them to do something, be a part of something, go somewhere. He had a sudden feeling that no one had done that before.

Then he knew what Brad was talking about. He was sitting at the table reserved for losers.

▪4▪

The First Run Is the Hardest

Rusty looked better on Saturday morning. When Scott went into the barn to feed him, the setter stood up and walked slowly across the stall, flying his ragged tail in a weak greeting.

"Look at you." Scott knelt down. "You're doing great."

"What did he do?" Howdy hurried in, carrying a pan of broth.

"He walked all the way over here. Oh, thanks, Howdy. Guess I forgot Rusty's breakfast."

"His leg must be a lot better. Can he go with us to workouts this morning?"

"He isn't a sled dog, Howdy. And he doesn't belong to us, anyway. But maybe we ought to take him outside now, so he can . . . you know."

"Yeah. Come on, Rusty." The dog limped ahead of them, out of the stall. "Do you think we'll get to keep him, Scott?"

"I don't know. Mom's picture of him was in the newspaper Wednesday, but maybe the owners don't get the paper. Or, maybe they're out of town."

"I hope they never come back." Howdy followed Rusty out of the barn.

Me, too, Scott thought. Me, too.

Kaylah and Bruno rounded the corner of the barn and hurried over to sniff at Rusty. I've got three dogs, Scott thought, savoring the idea.

For a second he could feel the sled gliding over the trail, hear the snow creak under the runners, see the finish line just ahead . . .

Then he stopped himself and shut off the movie in his mind. No, I haven't got three dogs. Only one of them is a sledder and the other two don't belong to me.

Sure, he could race with only Kaylah if he had to, but he'd be put in the peewee class, or at least the elementary events, with just one dog. That wasn't for him anymore. Dad had always fielded a big team, and so would he eventually.

There was something magical about training a bunch of dogs to pull together, Dad used to say. Train them to pull the way a family's supposed to. Together, in the same direction, helping each other, wanting the same thing.

"Scott, Howdy, come in to breakfast." Mom stood at the open back door.

"Come on," Howdy said, his eyes bright. "Your mom's cooking waffles this morning."

"Be right in, as soon as I put Rusty back in the barn." Scott watched Howdy hurry across the barnyard, his thinness hunched together in his heavy jacket, his head tucked down, away from the biting wind.

It had rained during the week, and now, as he waited for Rusty to finish, Scott looked up at the sky to see if there would be more. Pewter clouds hung like old gray kites on the line of the horizon, and pins of moisture pricked his cheeks. It felt almost like snow, and there was so much to do before the snow. Too much, he'd never be ready in time if he didn't start soon.

"Lookin' good," Scott said a few minutes later, patting Rusty's bony flanks. "You'll be the same as new one of these days."

Inside the barn he put down Rusty's bowl of broth, and kibble for Kaylah and Bruno, before he hurried into the house.

Howdy and Caroline were seated at the table, sloshing maple syrup on thick Belgian waffles.

Mom turned from the stove. "Got a hot one for you, Scott," she said. "Wash your hands and sit down."

He began to wash. "Where's . . . you know."

"Brad hasn't come down yet, and your dad went up to see what's keeping him."

Scott turned from the sink so quickly that water spilled onto the floor. "Mom, he isn't . . ."

"Scott," she said, a warning note in her voice. "Sit down and eat your breakfast."

He sat down, looked at Howdy and Caroline plowing through their waffles. If Howdy wasn't careful, he'd be as fat as Caroline before the end of next week. He acted as if he'd never had a square meal before.

Mom sat down with a cup of coffee. "Are you excited about the workouts today?" she asked. "Maybe there'll be someone there that we know."

"Don't see how." Scott shrugged. "Havre isn't exactly the sled-dog capital of the world."

"But they might have a very active club and attract mushers from all over the West." Mom got up to get another waffle.

"Are you gonna work out Kaylah today?" Caroline asked.

"No, I don't have a training cart, remember?"

"What's a training cart?" Howdy tipped his empty dish to spoon up some syrup.

"It's a three-wheel cart the dogs pull when there isn't any snow." Scott watched as Howdy began to butter the new waffle. Look at the amount he was taking, for crumb's sake. It was grease city around here.

"So what's the point of the cart then?" Howdy asked.

"More training time. Sled-dog teams don't just happen. They need to exercise and train—work up their endurance and speed."

"Just like human beings." Howdy began to eat, taking mammoth bites.

"It was my turn for the next waffle," Caroline said, staring at Howdy. "You went out of turn."

"No, I didn't."

"Yes, you did."

"Okay, simmer down, you two," Mom said. "Here's another one, Caroline."

Brad walked in from the hall, followed by his dad. Neither looked especially happy, but Mr. Hartfield was doing his best to keep a smile going.

"Look, Brad," he said. "Waffles this morning."

"I ate when I got up earlier." Brad walked over and reached for his jacket on a peg by the back door.

"Where are you going?"

"Thought I'd go over to Matt's."

"But we're all going to the workouts in Havre," Mr. Hartfield said.

"I can take care of myself." Brad zipped up his jacket. "I don't need you."

Mr. Hartfield came over to stand in front of Brad. "That

isn't the point, and anyway, I thought we had this straightened out upstairs. We're all going together."

Scott pictured the three dogs as he had left them, eating quietly together in the barn. They're doing a better job of getting along than we are, he thought.

By the time the six of them and Kaylah left, it was nearly ten o'clock. Scott sat in the very back of the station wagon with the dog, the wicker baskets of food, and Mom's photography bag. Twenty minutes later, they pulled up to a gas station in Box Elder.

"How long does it take to get to Havre?" Caroline asked as they waited for the station attendant.

"About an hour or so," Mr. Hartfield said, "unless we run into some weather, which might happen. Look at those clouds." He got out of the car and began to pump the gas himself.

Scott glanced out the window. Down home in Truckee, there'd be snow in clouds like that. Up here, he wasn't sure. Up here he wasn't sure about anything.

While Mr. Hartfield paid for the gas, a pickup truck pulled in to the pump across from them. Scott looked at the faces staring at him from the passenger window. Oh, shoot, there was that skinny girl, Michelle, and her sister. He'd sat with them in the cafeteria every day this week. Now here she was again, and trying to tell him something, too, mouthing words he couldn't hear.

Oh, well, he thought, as they drove down the highway a moment later. She'll tell me on Monday. What a motor-mouth.

By the time they arrived at the field just outside Havre, where the workouts were going to be held, the sky had begun to clear. The dogs could work after all. But Scott felt no surge of excitement, only a sense of emptiness. Suddenly he wished he'd stayed at the farm.

"What do we do now?" Mr. Hartfield was looking in the rear-view mirror at him.

Scott shrugged. "Watch some workouts, I guess."

Mr. Hartfield got out of the car. "Come on, everyone. This is going to be fun."

His voice sounded false to Scott. He thinks he's making points with me, but it won't work, Scott thought.

Howdy and Caroline jumped from the car and headed for a makeshift hot-dog stand.

"Don't buy anything," Mom called after them. "We're going to eat in a little while.

Scott let Kaylah out of the car and fastened him to a stake-out chain. He immediately began to pull at the end of it, jumping and barking at other staked dogs.

"Kaylah remembers what fun this is." Mom's voice sounded hollow, too, Scott thought. Why don't they leave it alone?

"Now what?" Brad stood next to Scott, looking at the people and the dogs milling around pickups and station wagons drawn together in a semicircle.

"Pretty soon workouts will get going," Scott said. "They've got a trail marked out over there." He pointed to some red flags heading over a short rise into a nearby field.

"Hello, folks, my name's Amos Underwood. I'm the referee." Scott turned around to look up at a giant of a man. Even his hands were the size of dirt movers, Scott thought, looking at the one outstretched to shake his own.

"Who's the musher in the crowd here?" Amos asked, his dark, gentle eyes looking at each of them.

"I am," Scott said, still mesmerized by Amos's size and

appearance. His thick, black hair flowed into a dark, wiry beard, giving him the appearance of one of those prophets Scott had heard about in Sunday School. All he needed to complete the picture was a long robe and sandals instead of the worn jeans and plaid shirt that covered his big frame.

"Good, I'll sign you up for a workout." Amos began to write on the paper fastened to a clipboard. "In the junior class."

"But I didn't bring a team."

"That Mally the only one you've got?" Amos pointed at Kaylah with his pencil.

"Yes. I just planned to watch." Suddenly Scott felt cold. He didn't want to do anything today, especially in front of Brad and Mr. Hartfield. Kaylah hadn't been in harness for a while now, and Scott hadn't worked out either. What if he really goofed it up?"

"No problem." Amos continued to write. "You can borrow two of my dogs. If your dog is conditioned to run in a team, he'll work fine with mine. My dogs are accepting."

"That's wonderful, Scott." Mr. Hartfield gave him a slap on the back. "You show me what to do to help get ready. Come on, give Brad a job, too."

Scott looked at Brad's face. He wanted a job helping about as much as he wanted a case of the hives.

"Need to borrow a cart?" Amos asked.

"Yes. Dad sold ours."

"How much did you get for it?" Amos was looking at Mr. Hartfield. Oh, crumb, he'd said it all wrong.

"I think Scott means . . . ," Mr. Hartfield began.

"He isn't my dad," Scott blurted out.

"Oh, I see." Amos nodded. "I misunderstood. I'll make sure that you get a cart so you can have a good workout."

Then he disappeared into the crowd milling around the starting line.

"It's okay, Scott." Mr. Hartfield put his arm around Scott's shoulders.

Scott eased out of his grasp and walked away to Kaylah. He's trying to be nice, but he's trying too hard, Scott thought. He stayed with Kaylah until, sometime later, he heard his name being called.

"Scott." Mom walked over to him, her camera hanging from a strap over her shoulder. "You're up in ten minutes."

He turned to see Amos waving him over to a cart and two dogs. Quickly he untied Kaylah from the stake-out line and led him over.

"I figured you'd want your own dog to lead," Amos said.

Scott looked down at the gang line fastened to the cart. Two beautiful Mallys, gray and white and eager, stared at him from wheel dog and point dog positions. Scott reached out his hand and they nosed it gently.

"Did I figure right?" Amos gripped his excited dogs tightly so they wouldn't take off with the cart.

Scott nodded. "Yeah, that's right." Get it over, he told himself. Remember, the first run of the year is always the hardest.

Quickly he fastened Kaylah into harness. It was clean, expertly mended, and fit Kaylah perfectly across his thick, muscled chest.

Amos handed over control of his dogs to Mr. Hartfield and gave the harness a quick inspection. "Strong dog," he said, giving Kaylah a quick hug. "You must give him plenty of muscle food." Then he pointed to the field. "You see the trail, don't you? Watch that first corner and after that, you should have no problem.

"Remember, you're running against time today and just for fun. Everybody's starting off at three minute intervals."

Scott nodded, unable to speak. His throat felt closed up, out for repairs. He couldn't talk, he could only remember, and barely at that, what he should do.

"Five, four, three, two, one," Amos shouted. "And, go."

Mr. Hartfield turned the dogs loose and they took off, barking and yapping. Scott held on to the handlebar and ran behind the cart to accelerate their speed. Then he jumped on as the dogs yanked the cart so hard he felt his neck jerk backward first, then forward. Scott pumped with one foot, and the dogs measured his rhythm with their own. Finally they fell into a racing lope that propelled him down the earthy track and up over the rise.

"Haw," he called, and the dogs turned quickly to the left, squaring the corner too soon, too fast. The cart tipped crazily and Scott felt his balance go, as well as his command of the dogs. They were running too hard and fast now. He had to bring them under control or they'd run themselves out and have nothing left after the first mile.

"Easy, easy," he called. "Go easy." Another corner came and the dogs slowed, gradually settling into a pace they could keep for the rest of the distance. Three miles, that was usual for a workout.

Suddenly the sun broke through the cloud covering. The sky was big, it was really big, just like the ads say about Montana. It must be bigger here than anywhere else.

"*Go, Scott.*"

Who was that? Mom? Caroline?

He rounded the three-quarter mark and headed back to the finish line. Now he pumped again, to help the dogs up a rocky incline. He was doing great, making good time.

The finish was just ahead, he saw everyone standing there, heard them yelling to bring the dogs on, felt the dogs pick up their speed for the last hundred feet before they rolled over the finish line. Wish Jamie could have seen this, Scott thought.

Mr. Hartfield hurried forward to grab Kaylah's harness and bring the dogs to a complete stop. Scott was glad for the help. His breath felt raspy in his throat, and sweat made him feel damp and prickly. He was way out of shape.

"Terrific, Scott," Mr. Hartfield yelled. "Really terrific."

Mom rushed up, clicking away with her Rolliflex. Howdy and Caroline ran up to pet the dogs.

"Good time," Amos shouted, coming toward him. "Practice cornering and you could win some races. Why don't you get three dogs together?"

"We already have three dogs, haven't we?" Mr. Hartfield said. "Haven't we, Brad?"

Brad jammed his hands in his jeans pockets and kicked at some gravel around his feet. "Bruno's not interested," he said.

He didn't have to add, neither am I. But Scott knew, and that was okay with him. Totally.

▪5▪

Whose Idea Is It Anyway?

Scott heard his name being called at first recess on Monday and didn't have to look around to see who it was.

"Hi Michelle," he said.

She grabbed at his arm, and he turned to look at her. She must have run all the way across the playground, because she was out of breath, her cheeks were flushed, and her funny-colored hair was messy.

"What's the matter, Michelle?" Scott asked. "Somebody chasing you?" He'd taken to teasing her a little; she seemed to like it, and it gave him something to say.

"You're so silly," Michelle said, her pink cheeks growing darker. "I want to show you something." She rattled a newspaper in her hand.

"Now let me guess. You want to show me a newspaper, right?"

"Will you be serious?" Michelle asked. Her little sister, Barbie, ran up now.

"Did you tell him yet?" Barbie asked. Then, without waiting for anyone to answer, she said, "We saw you Saturday, up at Havre, at the races. Dad took us because he had to go there to get two new tires for the tractor, so he said we could go with him. Then Michelle wouldn't leave, so Dad got mad. Mainly though because the tires cost so durn much."

"Wait a sec," Scott interrupted. "You came to the workouts?" Oh, no, what if Brad found out? What if Brad heard a girl came to see him run his dogs?

"Yes, we saw you," Michelle said. "Oh, Scott, you were absolutely terrific. I mean, it was just great. And look, your name was in Sunday's newspaper. It says you came in third place in juniors. See?" She held the paper so close to him he couldn't focus.

A sudden gust of wind nearly blew the paper away, and they both grabbed for it at the same time. Scott's arm tangled with hers; they tried to break free, but it only got worse. Now his arm was around her shoulder, and now his hand was touching hers. Michelle was so close, he could feel her bubble-gum breath on his cheek. How could this have happened?

Scott backed up quickly and looked around to see if anyone had seen them. But no one had. What a relief! Some guys from his class were gathered way over in a corner of the playground, tossing a ball back and forth. A few girls were standing near a teacher, listening to his instructions. Other kids milled around, kicking at tumbling leaves skittering across the hardtop.

"I have to go," Scott grumbled into his jacket collar. "See you later."

"But don't you want the paper?" Michelle began to run along beside him. "It's got your name in it."

"I know how to spell my name." She was like a tick—he couldn't shake her.

He kept walking, and finally he realized she wasn't running beside him any more. He turned around to see her looking after him with the newspaper still in her hand. Why did she have to look like that anyway?

Slowly he walked back. "I guess I'll take the paper home to show Mom," he said. "Thanks." He folded it up and stuffed it into his jacket pocket.

"Scott, can I come over and watch you train your dogs?" Michelle asked, walking along beside him again.

"There's not much to see," he answered. "I only have Kaylah and we're just going to jog together until there's snow."

"Kaylah." Michelle tried out the name. "What does it mean?"

"It means . . . it means king of the wolf pack," Scott said, feeling proud that he'd named Kaylah himself.

"It does?" Michelle asked. "What language is it?"

"Don't know for sure," Scott was forced to admit. "But I know that's what his name stands for."

"What are you going to do first?" Michelle asked. She was full of questions.

"Fix up my sled."

"Don't you have one of those cart things you used on Saturday?" Barbie bounced along on the other side of him now, and he felt as if he were drowning in girls.

"No, that belongs to Amos, the referee."

"You can borrow my wagon if you want to," Barbie said.

"Wagon?" Scott didn't want to borrow a kid's wagon for Kaylah to pull. What a crummy idea.

"We're just trying to help," Michelle said. "Why can't you use a wagon?"

"First of all, because there's no brake on it. I don't want my dog being run over by a wagon when he stops."

"Oh," Michelle said. "I guess that would be a problem. Can't you make one? A cart, I mean?"

Suddenly Scott was remembering. "I'll see you later, Michelle," he said, heading back to the school building. "I've got to get a pencil and a piece of paper."

Scott's mind was tumbling so fast he didn't even notice as Brad came up alongside him. "Hey, Scott, you lost something. Your groupies stopped following you."

"Beat it, Brad," he said, thinking hard, trying to picture something in his mind.

He finished his design during social-studies class. While everyone else was reading about the rainfall of the mid-western states, he was designing a plywood drag. He had seen them before, used by people who couldn't afford carts. He would build his *own* drag for Kaylah to pull.

Scott felt fairly confident with tools. He knew how to use a saw, and there wasn't much to building one of those things, just a piece of plywood, cut in a triangle, about two feet on each side, and then some two by fours . . .

Oh, wait a minute, where was he going to get that stuff? He didn't have much money; how could he buy the lumber if he didn't have money? Maybe someone would give him a job so he could earn some. But who? And what would he do? He was a twelve-year-old kid. Maybe Mr. Hartfield . . . But he hated the idea of asking him for anything. Money. Job. Anything. Unless Mom would do it for him.

After school Scott was the first one on the bus, as if his being there would make it start sooner. Come on, he said in his mind to the driver and the rest of the kids. Come on, let's split. I've got work to do.

Finally the bus started on its route, tortoise speed. Would

they never get to their stop? Ten miles suddenly seemed like ten thousand.

"How do you like school?" Caroline spoke beside him. How long had she been sitting with him? Had she spoken to him before?

"It's okay, I guess. How about you?"

"I've got a nice teacher," Caroline said, kicking her feet against the seat in front of them. "She asked me to tell about where I used to live, but I didn't want to."

Scott looked at her, surprised. Caroline never missed a chance to talk. "Why not?" He pulled at her red hair spilling over her jacket collar.

"Well, it's just because . . . because . . ." Suddenly she buried her face in Scott's jacket sleeve. "I get so lonesome for home when I talk about it."

Scott put his arm around her, thinking this was the second time he'd put his arm around a girl today. But this was different. Caroline was his sister. Putting an arm around her was like putting an arm around himself.

"Caroline," he whispered. "Know what I'm going to do?"

"What?" She pulled her face from its hiding place in his jacket. "What are you going to do?"

"Don't tell anybody yet. Especially not Brad."

"I wouldn't tell Brad anything," Caroline said, wiping her nose on her jacket sleeve. "I wouldn't tell him if his pants were on fire."

"Why?"

"Today, on the playground, he told me to get lost, permanently. What does permanently mean?"

"Forget him. Forget what he said."

"But Mom says we're a family now and we're supposed to

be nice. And my teacher says we're a bi-nuclear family. Does that mean we're gonna blow up?"

Scott laughed. "You're crazy, Caroline. Crazy, but nice. I don't know what your teacher meant—you'll have to ask Mom when we get to the farm."

"I hope it means that Brad will blow up." Caroline glanced to the back of the bus where Brad and Howdy were sitting. Then she was quiet the rest of the way to their stop, her interest in Scott's plans forgotten.

Mom was snapping a picture of Rusty sitting on the back steps as they walked into the barnyard.

"Look who's up and following me around," Mom called, pointing at Rusty with her light meter. "He's been outside with me most of the afternoon, so I thought I'd take another picture to send to the newspaper. The first one I took inside the barn was pretty dark. Maybe his owners didn't recognize him."

"He looks better than he did last week, anyway," Howdy said. "Probably his owners didn't know that old bag of bones was theirs."

"True," Mom said, smiling. "I baked some cookies this morning."

Howdy and Caroline raced up the steps and into the house.

"Was there any mail for me today?" Brad asked, making lines in the gravel with the toe of his boot. "From Billings?"

"No, Brad," Mom said. "Did you send away for something?"

"Not exactly. I was expecting to hear from someone, that's all." He shrugged in her general direction, then went inside.

"Where's Kaylah?" Scott asked.

"I saw him a few minutes ago." Mom pushed her dark, wavy hair away from her face and shaded her eyes as she looked around. "There he is. Kaylah has been with David most of the afternoon."

"What's Mr. Hartfield doing?" Scott looked to the north forty where he saw the tractor and flatbed wagon hitched to it.

"He's mending fences, checking the winter crop. There's so much to do here, even in winter."

Now would be a good time to talk to Mom about the plan to build a drag, Scott thought. Now, while Mr. Hartfield was busy somewhere else and Scott wouldn't have to talk to him.

"Mom, got a minute?"

"Sure, what's the matter? Did you have a problem with Brad today?"

"No, he's just his usual obnoxious self."

"Scott," Mom said. "Try to get along, okay? I was just wondering. He always seems so sad, so bothered about something."

Scott shrugged. "He'll get over it, whatever it is."

"What did you want to talk about, Scott?" Mom stood beside him, and he suddenly realized he didn't have to look up at her as much as he used to. That meant he'd been growing. At least something good was happening lately.

Quickly he told her about building a plywood drag, showed her his plans, how much lumber he'd need, and what he thought it would cost.

"I don't have any money, but I can pay you back a little at a time, out of my allowance."

"Why don't we talk to David about it?" Mom asked.

"I don't want to," Scott interrupted.

"But he might have the wood you need. He might be happy to give it to you."

"Mom . . ." Why didn't she understand?

"He seems so interested in you, Scott, and wants to help."

"Mom . . ." Scott tried again.

"I'm not going to argue about this, Scott. You talk to David tonight, when he comes in for supper."

The six of them sat down to Mom's fried chicken when Mr. Hartfield came in at five-thirty.

"How about this?" Mr. Hartfield said, looking around the table. He couldn't seem to stop grinning. "We got ourselves a family, Margaret."

"Please pass the chicken," Howdy said, in his get-on-with-it voice. Platters and bowls of chicken, potatoes, gravy, vegetables, and buttermilk biscuits were handed around. Howdy attacked his plate like a razorback in a beanfield.

Mom kept staring at Scott, trying out one of her meaningful looks on him. But he couldn't make words come out of his mouth. He just sat there, piling his potatoes into a mountain, putting in a gravy river around it.

"David," Mom said. "Scott has something he wants to talk to you about." She had that hurt look in her eyes, like Michelle had today. Crumb, he didn't know how to handle women at all.

"What's it about, Scott?" Mr. Hartfield was waiting. "About racing? I sure hope so."

Scott took a deep breath and began. By the time he finished, he knew Mr. Hartfield had already built the plywood drag in his head. It was already out of Scott's control, his say-so.

"Got plenty of spare lumber, Scott, and you're welcome to it." Mr. Hartfield spoke in his deep, booming voice. "We've got spare parts for everything on this ranch. You name it, we've got it."

"Thanks," Scott said.

"And when you need some help, let me know."

"That's okay."

"Brad's pretty good with a saw, too."

Scott looked at Brad, and their glances slid away from one another as if they'd been greased. Stop pushing, Scott thought. Stop pushing us at each other.

"What's a bi-nuclear family?" Caroline's voice interrupted the sudden silence.

"I guess it's sort of like ours," Mom said. "Parts of two families coming together to make one. Why do you ask?"

"My teacher said that's what Mr. Hartfield's family is now."

Mom smiled at Mr. Hartfield before she looked at Howdy. "How do you like the chicken, Howdy?"

"It's good," he answered, his mouth smeared with grease and crumbs. "The best I ever ate."

"Our mom makes good chicken, too," Brad said. "Don't forget."

"She always burned it." Howdy carefully selected another drumstick.

"She did not!" Brad glared at him. "Our mom did chicken just like this. Better."

"Burned it," Howdy said before taking another mammoth bite.

"You wart . . ."

"Brad," Mr. Hartfield's voice sounded a warning. "Everybody's entitled to his own idea."

"He shouldn't talk about Mom that way," Brad said. "You did it. You told him bad things about her."

"He did not." Howdy put down his fork. "Mom was always sitting around, painting squiggly lines to make pictures, and she let the chicken burn."

"No, she didn't. She was a good mom." Suddenly Brad was standing up.

"Sit down, Bradley," Mr. Hartfield said.

"I don't want any more. I'm through."

"It's all right." Mom's voice was so quiet. "You may be excused, Brad."

Brad bolted from the room just as Scott remembered. He was waiting to hear from his mom so he could move to Billings to be with her. But how long had it been since Brad had heard from her, anyway?

▪6▪

One Drag After Another

Scott walked slowly across the barnyard on Thursday afternoon after school. Mr. Hartfield was waiting in the barn, waiting to build the plywood drag with him. Man-to-man stuff, Mr. Hartfield called it when they had a talk yesterday.

Mr. Hartfield was always wanting to talk to him, but Scott just didn't know how. With Dad, you just went up and started talking; only with Mr. Hartfield it was different. And he already had his own boys, so why would he be interested in talking to a kid that wasn't his own?

Maybe he wanted to show Mom what a terrific guy he was, Scott thought. Yeah, he was probably trying to make points with her. They were so lovey-dovey, he probably would do that.

Scott stepped inside the barn door, and Rusty loped toward him. "Hey, boy, look at you." He knelt down to hug him, felt his coat grown thicker, the body underneath less bony and more rounded.

Mr. Hartfield stepped out of the tack room. "You're doing a good job with him, Scott." He wiped his greasy fingers on a stained rag.

"Everybody did it, not just me." Scott couldn't explain it, especially to himself, that he didn't even want to take a compliment from Mr. Hartfield. Taking anything from him seemed disloyal.

"You're right. Everybody helped." Mr. Hartfield kept wiping his hands, but they weren't getting any cleaner. Finally he said, "Are you ready to built that plywood contraption? I've got a piece of wood all laid out in here."

"Yeah, I brought my plan." Reluctantly Scott took the paper from his jeans pocket.

"Well, then." Mr. Hartfield hesitated.

Scott looked up at him, wondering. He was usually so sure of himself, knew just what to do every second.

"I don't quite know how to say this." Mr. Hartfield paused again.

Then Scott had it. "That's okay, Mr. Hartfield. I expect to pay you for the wood and anything else I use."

"No, no, Scott, you don't have to do that. It's just . . . it's just . . . I wish you'd call me David. I know you can't call me Dad yet, but at least call me David. Will you do that, Scott?"

Scott opened his mouth, but nothing would come out. *How can I promise to do that? It would make him closer, more like a dad, and he isn't. Not mine, anyway. It might seem like I'd forgotten my own.* "I . . . I . . ." Scott fought the cotton in his mouth. It choked off the words he wanted to say.

"It's probably too soon," Mr. Hartfield was saying. "But I want you to know it would make me feel good if you tried." He turned and went into the tack room. "Come on, Scott, let's build that drag."

Before Scott could follow, Brad came in.

"You got a letter," Brad said, giving him an envelope. His dark eyes looked longingly at it.

Scott stared at the envelope with the unfamiliar handwriting. Grandma's writing looked like snail trails and Jamie wasn't a person to write much. He ripped the envelope open.

"Scott, are you coming?" Mr. Hartfield's voice came from the tack room. Then he appeared in the doorway. "Oh, hi, Brad. Did you come to help?"

"No, I got homework to do." He started to leave.

"We could use you," Mr. Hartfield was saying. "Did you hear from California, Scott?"

"No, Amos Underwood wrote to me. He's that guy we met up at Havre."

"I remember him. Nice fella."

"He sent a schedule of races that are going to be held in Montana this winter. How far is Billings from here? The state club is going to have a big meet there just before Christmas."

"Billings is about . . ."

"It's two hundred and forty-three miles," Brad said.

Mr. Hartfield stared at him. "Where did you pick that up? School, maybe?"

"Yeah." Brad glanced at Scott, then looked away. But Scott got the message because he remembered. Brad was waiting for a letter from Billings. His mom. And now Brad was asking him to be quiet and not give it away. But why didn't Mr. Hartfield know about these plans of Brad's? That was a strange one.

"Come on, Scott," Mr. Hartfield said. "If we hurry and build that drag, you can try it out before dark."

"Guess I'll help, too," Brad said.

"Thought you had homework." His dad looked puzzled.

"It'll wait. What does this thing look like?" Brad walked ahead of Scott into the tack room.

"Show him your plan, Scott," Mr. Hartfield said. "I'll get the saw."

Scott spread out his paper on the workbench, and Brad stood beside him to look at it.

"Thanks," Brad whispered under his breath.

"It's okay," Scott said, wanting to ask, but not daring to.

It didn't take them long to build the drag, especially with Brad working on it. He had a knack for using tools that Scott envied.

"That's neat," Scott said later, when they'd finished. "Maybe you'd help me with my sled, too."

"I could probably do that," Brad said. He looked around and saw that his dad had gone outside. "If I'm here," he added.

"Right," Scott nodded. "If you're here."

Scott walked outside to the barnyard and began to attach the brake to the drag, but he couldn't get it to catch just right.

Brad wandered over to watch. "What's the problem?" He stuffed his hands into the back pockets of his jeans.

"Don't know." Scott stood up and looked around, wondering if he could bring himself to ask Mr. Hartfield for help. "But I'd better get it fixed before I hook Kaylah to it."

"I don't know why you're so particular. Your dog probably wouldn't even feel it if that drag hit him."

"It could hurt him plenty and spook him besides." Scott felt his hands curl into fists as he stared at Brad. "If you think it's nothing, let's hook up Bruno. Let's see how he likes getting socked with it."

"No," Brad yelled. "All you want to do it get your hands on my dog so you can have a team. That's all you think about."

"Me?" Scott yelled back. "I wouldn't have your dumb dog on any team of mine. It's your dad who keeps shoving him at me. Tell him to lay off."

"You tell him. If you don't, he'll take over."

"So I noticed." Scott felt like taking a punch at someone and it might as well be Brad. Why did he suddenly get so steamed up anyway? He was being halfway decent until he blew up.

Then Scott remembered how Brad had looked at the letter from Amos.

"Maybe you'll hear from her tomorrow," he said quietly, almost in a whisper.

Brad turned quickly to look at Scott and finally let out a long, stored-up breath. "Yeah, maybe." He walked over to the drag. "You want some help?"

"I could use it." Scott watched while Brad worked with the brake. He's got brains in his fingers, Scott thought. He knows just what to do. Like Jamie. He knew what to do, too.

Fifteen minutes later Brad stood up and jammed his hands back into his pockets. "Your dog won't get hit in the behind now."

"Thanks, Brad," Scott said.

"No sweat," he answered and walked away.

Every now and then he acts like a human being, Scott thought. Sometimes I could almost like him. But only sometimes.

Mom announced at the supper table that night that all

the boys in the family had to get haircuts tomorrow. No amount of arguing changed her mind and Scott was still fuming as he walked downtown to Box Elder with Brad and Howdy the next afternoon after school.

It wouldn't take them long to get to the barber's, Scott thought as they walked to the business district. What there was of it huddled all around the square.

The Feed and Seed squatted on one corner across from the post office. J. C. Penney's, where they had to meet Mom later, occupied another corner. A grocery store and café leaned against each other a few doors down, and a hardware store after that. Not much else except the barber shop.

Scott scuffed his feet in the fallen leaves on the sidewalk. There was no decent place for kids to hang out if they got the chance, no place to eat decent food like pizza or tacos. Shoot, they'd probably never heard of tacos up here.

"This is a real drag," Brad said, smoothing back his dark, scruffy hair. "I don't need a haircut."

"Me, either." Scott looked at Brad and grinned at his use of the word. They had that in common at least. Two kinds of drag.

"Dad said we had to do what she told us." Howdy spoke up on the other side of Scott. "Your mom's a good cooker, but sometimes she gets weird ideas."

"I know." Scott agreed. Like moving to Montana.

"My mom said it didn't matter about unimportant stuff like haircuts and I could do what I wanted about it." Brad crossed the street ahead of them.

"She sounds pretty neat," Scott answered. "I'll bet you didn't have to take showers every day when she was here."

"Every day?" Howdy practically yelled it and several old men, sitting on a bench in front of the feed store, turned to stare at them. "You mean that's next?"

Scott nodded. "Afraid so. She just wants to get to know you better before she lays that one on you."

"I wish I knew where Mom was," Howdy said. "I'd move there."

"Don't you . . . ," Scott began. Then he stopped. Howdy didn't know where she was either. Double weird, he thought, walking into the barber shop behind Brad and Howdy.

Scott stalled around and was the last one into the barber chair. He hated feeling trapped by the big apron draped all over him and being on total display in the picture window facing the square.

"So how do you like Montana?" the barber asked as he began to snip away at Scott's hair.

"It's okay." Why couldn't he hurry? Scott wondered. Cut the conversation and concentrate on the hair.

"What grade are you in?" the barber went on.

"Sixth." Oh, no, who was that girl coming down the street? Oh, jeez, there were a couple of other girls with her. If they saw him . . .

Scott turned quickly, but it was too late. Michelle had seen him. Now she stopped in front of the window and waved. The other girls were waving, too. All three were standing there like nerds, waving.

Brad and Howdy began to snicker behind him. "Look at your groupies, Scott," Brad said in an itsy-bitsy voice. "Wave to your fans, man."

"Knock it off," Scott said, wishing he could punch him. It

was bad enough to endure Michelle, but Brad didn't have to make it worse.

"Be still my heart," Brad said, doing a fainting act. Howdy walked over to the window and began to make faces until the girls backed away. After one last wave at Scott, they headed for J. C. Penney's.

"Wait till I tell the guys," Brad said, picking up a copy of *Sports Illustrated.*

"If you tell, I tell," Scott said, flaming.

"Tell what?" Howdy asked, turning around quickly.

"Nothing." Brad's voice held a warning. "He's just kidding, aren't you, Scott?"

Suddenly it was so quiet in the barber shop that the scissors sounded like a giant cricket. Snip, snip, snip, pause. Snip, snip, snip, pause.

On the way home Mom bubbled over with talk. "So I took the new pictures of Rusty into the newspaper office," she said. "And guess what?"

"What?" Caroline asked. "Do they know whose dog he is?"

"No," Mom answered. Scott saw her eyes in the rearview mirror. They were sparkly, full of fun. "They asked me if I wanted to take pictures for them on a regular basis, cover special events around town, that sort of thing."

"When do they ever have special events around here?" Scott asked. "When the bell rings in the church steeple?"

"Scott, don't talk like that," Mom answered. "I was thinking about the sled-dog races and I told Mr. Baker about them. He's the editor and he seemed very interested. Maybe I'll take a picture of you and the dogs for the paper."

"Spare me," Scott said.

"You should have been at the barber shop today," Howdy broke in. "You could have taken a picture of Scott and all his girlfriends."

"Come on, Howdy," Scott said. "Cut it out."

Caroline turned around from the front seat, her round face split in half by a grin. "Have you really got a girlfriend?"

"Maybe you and Brad have got secrets, but not me," Howdy went on. "I can talk about anything I want to."

Scott caught Mom staring at him in the rear-view mirror as they sped along the highway. He knew what she was doing; she was asking what secrets he had, especially with Brad. They hadn't exactly gotten off to a buddy-buddy start. But he wouldn't tell. No way did he want to get into that stuff about Brad's mom.

Twenty minutes later Mom turned into the long drive-way to the ranch and eased up by the mailbox.

"I'll do it," Brad said, hopping out of the car. He opened the red mailbox shaped like a miniature barn. Across the top David Hartfield's name was spelled out in wrought-iron letters. David Hartfield. No mention that any McClures lived here.

Brad looked through the envelopes in his hand before he returned to the car. "It's all for you and Dad," he said, handing the envelopes to Mom.

Now she glanced through them. "Oh, look, here's one from Truckee," she said.

"Is it from Grandma?" Caroline asked, looking over Mom's shoulder.

"No, it's from the Wagners." Mom ripped open the envelope. "Maybe they've had their baby." She began to read, then said, "Guess what?"

Brad groaned and Scott didn't blame him. More of Mom's guessing games. "They had triplets, right?" Scott asked.

"No, Mr. Wagner is coming to see us," Mom said, continuing to read. "He'll be here sometime over the weekend."

Scott sat back on the car seat and smiled. Mr. Wagner, Dad's old friend. His old sled-dog-racing buddy. It would be great to see him, talk about dogs and racing and snow. It would be just like it used to be, just . . .

No it wouldn't. It would never be the way it used to be. Couldn't he ever get that through his head?

▪7▪

Waiting For Mr. Wagner

Scott hurried out of the house after breakfast on Saturday morning. The weekend had finally come and Mr. Wagner would be coming with it. He'd called from Great Falls last night to say he'd arrive this afternoon around four.

Now, more than ever, Scott wanted to get Kaylah out for another run with the drag so he could show Mr. Wagner how well they'd been training. Maybe Mr. Wagner would have some advice to give him. He'd been champion so many times, almost as many as Dad.

As Scott fastened Kaylah to the drag, he wondered again about Mr. Wagner's visit. Why was he coming? It sure was out of the way.

Scott gave Kaylah extra weights to pull this morning, then released the brake and let him go. Quickly they ran to the north meadow behind the barn. The extra weights didn't slow Kaylah for a second; he pulled easily and barked himself silly, besides.

Bruno ran, too, barking in answer to Kaylah. Rusty followed, though running well behind. But he was gathering strength each day even if it would be a while before he could do any serious running.

What a team they'd make, Scott thought, watching the three dogs, admiring the beauty of their being together. If only . . . if only all three of them belonged to me.

Scott sighed as he ran beside Kaylah, feeling damp air brush his cheeks. No use thinking about having my own team for a few years, he thought. I'll just have to use Kaylah and a couple of pickup dogs. Maybe Amos will let me borrow his again. But I'm going to race. I'm going to race again.

Scott loosened the zipper of his lightweight jacket, feeling warm already, even though the air was cool. Now he looked at the slate-colored sky. Clouds, with soft edges to them, looked puffy full. They'd dump their rain before tonight.

By the time Scott returned forty-five minutes later, he was sweating hard and the dogs were panting as they went inside the barn.

They sound like a locomotive, Scott thought, easing Kaylah out of harness. The dog threw himself beside his bowl of water and began to lap quickly. Bruno and Rusty looked like a couple of kids, waiting in line behind him.

Mr. Hartfield stepped into the stall opening. "Have a good run?"

"Great," Scott managed to say.

"Wonder if you'd have time to give Brad some help with the horses?" Mr. Hartfield asked, petting Rusty now.

"Sure." Scott tried to sound interested, but he really wanted to work on his sled some more. He had so many things to ask Mr. Wagner.

"The horses haven't been exercised for the last couple of days, so we need to get them out for some trail time before the storm hits. Brad's hitching up his Appy right now, and you can take the quarter. I'll follow along in a few minutes with mine."

Scott walked into the stall where the quarter horse waited, wondering if a horse was anything like a dog to harness up.

Brad hurried in and took a bridle and bit from a peg on the wall. "Ginger, here, is a lot older than Georgia O'Keefe and doesn't have as much pep either. He's a good horse for a dude like you to ride." He worked as he spoke.

"I've ridden horses before." Scott got hot inside. Brad didn't have to call him a dude. But he was secretly relieved that Brad had started the bridle and bit, and finally the saddle. Scott noticed a kind of belt thing hanging under the horse's stomach. It was attached to the saddle so it must fasten here, on this side.

"You'd better cinch up the girth belt tighter than that," Brad began. "You can't fool old Ginger and . . ."

"Stop telling me what to do every second," Scott said. "The way you talk, you'd think I'd never seen a horse before."

"All right, all right." Brad put his hands up in the air in surrender. "You want to do it your way, so go ahead."

They worked in silence a moment before Scott asked, "Who's Georgia O'Keefe?"

"My horse." He leaned against Ginger's neck. "She's named for Mom's favorite artist."

"Did your mom give the horse to you?"

"Kind of. Georgia was Mom's special horse before . . . before she went away. When she decided not to come back, she wrote and said that I could have Georgia." Brad paused and Scott waited, feeling his need to say more. "I'll bet Mom misses her though. I'll bet she'd like to have Georgia back."

Brad led Ginger from the stall and Scott followed them outside. Georgia O'Keefe was tied to the handle of the barn door, waiting.

Without speaking, Brad and Scott mounted up and the horses moved off at a brisk trot. Scott tried to relax, but his grip on the reins was white-knuckled. The back of a horse was so much higher off the ground than the runners of a sled. And bumpier besides.

"Where are we headed?" Scott asked a few minutes later when he could think of something else besides his sore butt.

"Toward the north meadow."

"In the direction of the mountains?"

"Right. I used to ride out this way a lot, and once I went up there into the pass."

"You really know the territory."

"It's easy when you've lived here all your life."

Scott glanced up at the low-lying range crouching on the horizon. Its look was totally different from the Sierra peaks at home. Rather than being pointed and ragged edged, these mountains looked as if they'd been shaped with a spoon, maybe a giant ice cream scoop.

"What range is that?"

"Bear Paw mountains. Not really all that high, but you can ski in them. Our family used to go together a lot. All of us."

Brad paused, but it was like the time before, in the barn. Scott knew he had more to say, that he'd chosen Scott to say these things to, as if Brad realized how much Scott had struggled with similar memories of his own.

Either he's finally decided I'm a human being, just like him, Scott thought, or he's setting me up for something. I wonder which it is?

"How far is it up to the pass?"

"Maybe five or six miles."

"Did you drive up that way when you went skiing?"

"There's no road from here. You have to go on horseback or hike. When we went skiing, we took the hard road to the other side of the mountain."

"Must be pretty neat."

"Nothing like it." Brad gave Georgia a nudge and she took off suddenly, following the fence line along the meadow's edge. Ginger followed, lunging quickly, and Scott felt himself slip sideways off her back. Something was wrong.

"Whoa, stop," Scott yelled. Ginger stopped, but Scott didn't. Grabbing for Ginger's thick mane, he tried to slow his fall, but the saddle slipped crazily to Ginger's side and dumped Scott to the hard ground.

For a moment he was too stunned to move or speak. He sat on his cold rear, clutching clumps of meadow weed as if that would stop his head from pounding.

Then he heard Brad and Georgia returning, and he struggled to get up. So far everything worked, but barely.

"What happened?" Brad asked, leaning down to look at him.

"That darn saddle slipped." Scott brushed himself off, then glared at Ginger. "How could that be?"

"Old Ginger played you for a fool and had his belly all puffed out when you cinched up his girth belt." Brad sounded as if he was giving a speech or something. "He made it nice and loose for himself the way he likes it."

"How do you know that?"

"I saw him do it, back in the barn."

"Why didn't you tell me?" Scott was really blazing now. "I could have been killed."

"I tried to, but you were Mr. Know-It-All, remember?"

Scott remembered, all right. "But you could have said something anyway. Especially if my life was in danger."

"Your life in danger?" Brad yelled back. "Mine was in danger, too, the way you were coming at me." Now he hopped off Georgia. "Here, let me show you." He began to work at the girth belt, tightening it around Ginger's belly.

"Thanks," Scott managed to say when Brad had finished.

"No sweat," Brad answered. "Do you want to quit?"

"No."

"Okay, okay." Brad was trying hard not to smile and Scott knew it. "So let's go."

Scott was still fuming as he climbed back on Ginger, but he tried to think of other things now. He knew that what had happened was his own fault. He only hoped that Brad wouldn't broadcast it all over school on Monday.

Kaylah and Bruno suddenly appeared beside them, running easily to keep the pace.

"Look who's caught up with us," Scott yelled, watching Bruno pace Kaylah. Dogs were something he knew about, and he knew Bruno showed plenty of strength for pulling a sled. His shoulder muscles were building nicely and Scott would love to hitch him up with Kaylah. But he couldn't, not without Brad's say-so.

Brad pulled Georgia O'Keefe to a halt at a promontory point near the edge of the path. Scott hadn't realized how steadily they'd been climbing until he looked back at the house and barn below. From here they looked doll-sized.

"No wonder I didn't know about the pass into the mountains," Scott said. "You can't see it from down there."

"When you know how to ride better, maybe I'll take you all the way up," Brad said.

"I could probably handle it right now." Scott's temper flared inside him again.

Brad looked around at the sky. "Too chancy today."

"You said you rode up there once by yourself?"

"Well, I wasn't totally alone," Brad said. "I was with my mom."

Scott felt a quickening inside. Why was Brad talking so much about his mom? Must be this place, he decided. Everything reminds him. It sure hasn't got anything to do with me.

"Like Howdy said, Mom is an artist and she likes to paint scenery best. One day she wanted to ride up to the top of the mountain and paint the view, so she asked me to come along because she's afraid of snakes."

"So what happened?"

"Nothing. She painted all day and I went exploring. I found this old falling-down cabin that must have belonged to a prospector a long time ago."

"Yeah, we've got a bunch of those in California left over from the Gold Rush."

The wind stirred suddenly around them, and the horses shifted uneasily on the path. "We'd better turn around," Brad said. "That storm is just about here."

Scott nosed Ginger around to the right. "Gee," he yelled automatically and Kaylah turned sharply right at the word. "Good dog," Scott said. "Mr. Wagner's gonna be impressed with you."

The clouds settled around them like old gray blankets and Scott snuggled deeper into his jacket. He was glad that he'd grabbed his knit cap at the last second.

He felt needles of wetness on his cheeks now, sharp and icy at first, then softening gradually to a more gentle touch.

"Hey, Brad," he yelled. "It isn't raining, it's snowing."

"I noticed." Brad zipped up his jacket. "Pardon me if I don't go into orbit, but I've seen a lot of snow."

"Does it always snow this early in November?"

"Sometimes we have snow for Halloween," Brad said. By the time spring comes it's pretty old stuff."

Would this be the time to say something? Scott wondered. "Maybe you'd feel different if you raced sled dogs," Scott said.

"Well, I don't. I've just got Bruno, who's your average dog with a mouth on one end and a tail on the other."

"He's strong enough to pull a sled." Scott felt he was pushing his luck saying that.

"How do you know?"

"I've been watching him. Maybe he could train with Kaylah, just for the fun of it."

"No, that's your department." Brad looked off toward the mountains. "Maybe, though, I'll go to some of races, just for the fun of it." Then he nudged Georgia O'Keefe and she began to lope, pulling ahead of Ginger on the trail.

Like the one down in Billings, Scott thought. I know you'll go to that one.

The horses understood they were going home now and strained hard at their bridles. Scott felt Ginger's eagerness gather under him as they cut through the meadow and sliced neatly through the chilly wind. Scott kept his head down, chin tucked into his collar, wishing he had gloves for his brittle fingers.

He saw Kaylah range up beside him, then hurry past and stop as they came to the ridge just before the land dipped into the barnyard. Kaylah paused, nose up, tail in a perfect circle above his sturdy back.

"Lookin' good, Kaylah," Scott called, wishing Mom was here with her camera.

Suddenly Kaylah bounded down ahead of him. He'd seen something. What? A jackrabbit, driven to cover under the brush?

Scott stared hard, past the snow that spat in his face, and then he saw what had excited Kaylah.

"Chinook! It's Chinook!" he yelled. "Come here, boy."

The great giant of a dog ran toward them, a kaleidoscope of black and silver flashing through the driving snow. He and Kaylah bounded together in a tangled frenzy, rolling, leaping, jumping together.

"Hey, Brad," Scott yelled. "Mr. Wagner's here." He kicked Ginger into a trot, wishing he dared to gallop the horse. Now, maybe, he'd find out why Mr. Wagner had come to visit them, and why he'd brought Chinook, who was only the best lead dog in the world—after Kaylah.

•8•

A Stunning Surprise

By the time Scott rode into the barnyard, Mr. Wagner had already gone into the house. But Chinook and Kaylah were still playing, wrestling like a couple of kids on the wet ground.

"Chinook," Scott yelled, jumping off Ginger and running toward the dogs. "Come here, Chinook."

Even though Scott braced himself, he was nearly knocked flat by the huge Mally's greeting. He felt the dog's slobbery tongue lick his face, its mouth pull at his clothes, eager and ready for a game.

Scott saw Brad coming out of the barn. "Hey, Brad, come over and meet Chinook."

"Not me," Brad answered, but he came over anyhow. "I don't want to get licked to death. Say, do you plan to let Ginger go to town by himself?"

Scott glanced up. He'd forgotten about him, and the old nag was taking advantage of it. He was headed toward the hard road. "Oh, sorry, Brad, I forgot."

Scott ran after the horse, and Kaylah and Chinook joined in as if it were a workout. After a moment Bruno followed and then Rusty, nearly keeping up.

It's like old times, Scott thought, running with the pack of them in the snow. These dogs run for the fun of it. Look at the way Kaylah and Chinook keep pace with one another. They're great. They're super. They could lead a winning team. My team.

Scott stopped suddenly. Why had Mr. Wagner brought Chinook? he wondered. Was he going to sell him to someone? Then why can't that someone be me? Oh, man, what a deal if I could buy that dog. But what would I use for money? There's always that blasted problem.

"Come on, you old oat eater," Scott said, grabbing Ginger's bridle and dragging reins. "Don't you know where you belong after all this time?"

Scott hurried Ginger back into the barn, removed his bridle and bit, threw his blanket over him, and tossed him a measure of hay before hurrying to the house. But all the while, he couldn't stop thinking about Chinook and some way that he could own him.

Scott raced up the back steps, stomped snow from his boots, and opened the back door. Mom, Mr. Hartfield, and Mr. Wagner were talking in the kitchen. They turned as he came in.

Then Scott was shaking Mr. Wagner's hand and, after that, gasping in an eye-popping hug. Man, the guy was strong. Scott had forgotten. He must eat his dog's muscle food.

"Would you look at the size of you?" Mr. Wagner stepped back and ran a hand through his thinning brown hair. "You've grown a foot since I saw you in September."

"How are you doing, Mr. Wagner?" Scott suddenly felt shy about the rush of emotions flooding him. "Have you seen Kaylah?"

"Not yet." Mr. Wagner threw his burly arms around Scott's shoulders again. "You first. Tell me how you're doing? Are you running Kaylah? Have you got a team yet?"

"No, not yet." Scott felt Mr. Hartfield and Brad looking at him, listening to each word. "But maybe soon. I was going to ask you . . ."

"We're all going to help, aren't we, Brad?" Mr. Hartfield took over with his booming voice. "Brad's got a dog and we found another one, so we'll have a team in no time. Maybe you'd take a look at the dogs and tell us what to do."

"Sure, be happy to." Scott felt Mr. Wagner's arm tighten around his shoulders, as if he were communicating a message through it. "Though I think you've got an expert right here, in this boy. He's pretty good, you know."

"Oh, I know that," Mr. Hartfield answered quickly. "I know he's good. Why don't we have some coffee and talk about what we have to do to get a team ready?" Mr. Hartfield led Mr. Wagner over to the table and pulled out a chair for him. "Have we got any pie left from last night, Margaret?"

"I made an extra one, but you're going to spoil a good supper if you eat pie now." Mom brought cups and a coffeepot to the table.

"Well, what about it?" Mr. Hartfield leaned forward and looked intently at Mr. Wagner. "Don't you think the boys could do something with the dogs we have?"

"It's possible." Mr. Wagner rubbed his chin, and the stubble of his beard sounded like sandpaper scraping his hands. "I'd have to look at them together before I passed judgment."

"Bruno's a real strong dog," Mr. Hartfield said. "Isn't he, Brad?"

"As strong as Scott's mutt," he answered. "And just as big, too."

"That's good." Mr. Wagner looked quickly from Brad to Scott and back again. "But you really need to have dogs matched for strength and endurance as well as size. You wouldn't want to have one dog who'd hold up the rest."

"Bruno wouldn't do that." Brad's eyes were hot, dark bits of coal.

"I'm sure he wouldn't," Mr. Wagner said. "I'm sure he's a fine dog."

Mr. Wagner knows how to handle people as well as dogs, Scott thought.

Then Mr. Wagner began to spin his yarns about sledding and races that he'd entered and often won. Scott felt wrapped in a time warp, remembering the comfort of other moments such as this, as the words painted beautiful dreams of dogs and sleds and snow.

"Did I tell you about the time I wanted to win so much that I misjudged the energy of my team, Scott?" Mr. Wagner asked.

He didn't wait for an answer, there wasn't supposed to be one. But Scott listened carefully, knowing there was a message especially for him in the story. Mr. Wagner was like that. Just like . . . just like Dad.

"It happened in this race, see, where I was supposed to be a big-shot musher. Everyone figured me to win. Anyway, when we were climbing a hill, I let go of the sled so my dogs wouldn't have to pull any extra weight. Before I could stop them, they pulled away from me and were over the top of the hill and out of sight. I had to chase them for five miles and those were the longest five miles of my life, I can tell you. And, of course, I lost the race."

Mr. Wagner's laughter flowed like rich molasses through the warm kitchen that smelled of roast beef simmering in the oven. Sometime, during the story, Caroline and Howdy had drifted in and stood, transfixed, near the doorway. Even Brad looked dreamy-eyed as he waited for Mr. Wagner to continue.

"I guess this is what I'm trying to say," Mr. Wagner said after a long pause. "People are going to give you all kinds of advice, and dogs are going to figure they know twice as much about running as you do because they've got twice as many legs. But Scott, you can't ever let go of control to others the way I let go of that sled."

I hear you, Scott thought. Dad used to say that, too. It's your race, all the way.

"You got a way with words," Mr. Hartfield said after a moment.

"I think I know what I'm talking about." Mr. Wagner twisted his empty cup between his hands. "And I like what I'm doing."

"You make it sound so exciting." Mr. Hartfield said. "Doesn't he, Brad?"

"Yeah," Brad said softly.

Scott looked at him, surprised. Did he mean he was becoming interested in sledding? That would be different. Or was he thinking about what Mr. Wagner had said and applying it to himself? That would be interesting, too.

But now Scott shook himself free of all other thoughts. He had to talk to Mr. Wagner about Chinook. Alone. And soon.

"Mr. Wagner, do you suppose you could look at my sled?"

"Don't be too long," Mom said, hurrying around the kitchen. "Supper's going to be ready soon."

"Good idea, Scott," Mr. Hartfield said. "Come on, let's go."

Mr. Hartfield grabbed his jacket from the peg by the door and his boys followed. How was Scott going to get a private talk with Mr. Wagner now? No way was he going to talk about buying Chinook in front of them. Mr. Wagner said take control and he was trying. But it would be easier if he didn't have to wrestle Mr. Hartfield for it.

Before Mom called them back into the house for supper, Mr. Wagner had inspected the sled with his expert eye. Then he'd offered advice that everyone followed without question. More bracing here, he said. And Mr. Hartfield added an extra bolt. Reglue this crack on the handlebar and clamp it until the epoxy sets, Mr. Wagner instructed.

Scott held the pieces of wood steady while Brad carefully worked them together. It was perfect, no seam showed to indicate there had been a break. Scott could see that Brad worked well with his hands and that he liked the feel of the wood, which was satiny to the touch.

He and Dad would have liked each other, Scott realized suddenly. The thought stunned him; he couldn't take his mind from it no matter how hard he tried.

Later, no one talked much at the table. Instead, they dug into the food and ate in happy silence, especially Mr. Wagner. When Mom brought out the apple and raisin pies for dessert, he had a second piece.

"Margaret, you're just as good a cook as Alice," he said, leaning back in his chair and sighing.

"How is Alice?" Mom asked. "And all the children?"

"We're doing fine now that I've found a job again," he said. "Don't know if you remember how the logging business went all to pieces down in Truckee."

"Yes, I remember," Mom answered quietly.

"We had some hard times," Mr. Wagner said. "I couldn't find work anywhere. But I finally found this job up in Canada, and things are only going to get better for the Wagners from now on."

"Canada?" Scott asked. "You're moving to Canada? You ought to get in some good racing up there."

"That's right," Mr. Wagner said. "The only problem is I had to sell my dogs, all but Chinook. Couldn't afford to feed them."

Now, Scott thought. Now, maybe I can find out about Chinook. "Are you thinking about selling Chinook in Canada?" he asked hesitantly. "Bet you could get a good price for him there."

Mr. Wagner looked at Scott before he spoke. "Chinook isn't for sale, son. I couldn't do that. Chinook isn't anybody I could ever sell."

Scott nodded, understanding how he felt. Of course. He should have known that Mr. Wagner would never sell his favorite dog. But a deep sadness flooded him as hopes of adding Chinook to his own team faded. Now what was he going to do?

"George, when you talk to Alice, please give her a message for me," Mom said. "Tell her that I'm very, very happy." Then she looked at Mr. Hartfield. Scott saw that it was a private look between them only and turned away.

"I can see that," Mr. Wagner smiled.

"What time do you want to get up in the morning?" Mom's face looked all pink and shiny. "I know you want to be on the road early."

"Don't you worry about it." Mr. Wagner stood up. "I'll just get up at first light and be on my way."

"There'll be coffee to heat if you want it," Mom said. "And some rolls. I'll make some sandwiches for you to take along."

Scott went to bed, leaving the grownups still at the table, talking. Tomorrow morning he'd get up and say his own private goodbyes to Mr. Wagner and Chinook.

I couldn't have bought Chinook anyway, Scott thought, just before he fell asleep. Mr. Wagner needs money right now, and that's just what I don't have plenty of.

Scott shook himself out of sleep at first light, trying to remember why he'd wanted to wake up this early. Then he heard the sound of a pickup revving its motor and knew.

Oh, shoot, he thought, running across the cold floor and opening the window.

"Mr. Wagner, wait," he called.

But the pickup was already roaring out of the barnyard, and Scott watched as it headed toward the hard road. When it was out of sight, he shut the window and shivered his way back to bed.

Then he heard something else. The dogs seemed to be all stirred up. What was going on? Maybe he'd better have a look and simmer them down before they woke up Mom and Mr. Hartfield.

Quickly Scott pulled on clothes over his pajamas and tiptoed downstairs and into the kitchen. He turned on the light and blinked for a second or two until he could see.

Mr. Wagner had left his coffee cup and plate on the table, and something else. It looked like a note. Scott walked over and picked it up.

"Dear Scott," the note began. "I told you Chinook wasn't for sale, and he isn't. But he is something else. He's a gift to you in honor of the friendship I shared with your father.

Chinook will enjoy running with you and Kaylah. Run well together. Your friend, George Wagner."

Scott dropped the note and ran out of the house, feeling the cold air knife his lungs. He ran across the barnyard, pulled open the barn door, turned on the light and ran to the stall. Kaylah and Chinook sat inside by the sled, yipping and yapping together, as Bruno and Rusty listened.

Mallys talk to one another, Scott remembered. And right now, Chinook was doing most of the talking, probably asking all kinds of questions about his new home.

▪9▪

The Fight of the Week

Snow continued to fall during the week. Each morning Scott woke to more of it and knew he could work with the dogs again after school that day.

Sometimes the snow had fallen as softly as baby powder. Other days it was as hard and crunchy as rock candy. There were so many shapes, so many sizes, so many kinds: wet, powdery, icy. So many kinds of snow. Which was really the best?

It's all good, Scott thought, as he dressed for school on Thursday morning. Each snowfall combined to tamp and pack the base he and the dogs needed to run.

When was the big race in Billings? he suddenly wondered. Quickly Scott searched around in the pile of papers on his dresser. It was here, somewhere. Oh, yeah, Amos's letter right here said December tenth. Good. That gave him a month or so, but he'd better send in his entry this weekend.

There was a soft knock on the door before it opened. "Mom says for you to hurry up," Caroline said. Her hair was more or less combed this morning, and her clothes actually seemed to match.

Caroline was usually out to lunch before breakfast, Scott

thought. But once in a while she surprised him and looked and acted normal. Suddenly he started to smile at his own thought.

"What's so funny?" Caroline demanded, following him around his room.

"Big secret," Scott said, searching for his jacket under the pile of clothes he'd worn yesterday.

"See if I care whether you tell me or not," Caroline said, walking around and touching things. "You sure have a messy room."

"Keep your crummy hands off," Scott said. "I know right where stuff is."

"Including your love letters from Michelle?"

"What are you talking about?"

"Howdy said Michelle is your girlfriend and he bets you and her write love letters back and forth." Caroline giggled and began to pick at a fingernail.

Scott's face felt hot. "Tell Howdy to mind his own business."

"Boy, you ought to see your face," Caroline said. "Wait till I tell Howdy."

"Don't you tell him anything."

"He says you and Brad have a secret, and it must be about girls." Now Caroline began to paw through some papers scattered across his desk. "And if you don't tell me, I'm going to tell Mom and him. You know, Mr. Hartfield . . . David."

"You're calling him David?" Scott whirled around.

"He asked me to, and it seemed a lot easier than always saying Mr. . . ."

"But you can't."

"Why not?"

Scott couldn't think of an answer he felt she'd understand. In fact, it was still so complicated to him that he couldn't sort it out. The word he thought of before, disloyalty, kept coming back to him. And he couldn't be disloyal to Dad, not now, not ever.

Scott walked over to the window and looked at the barnyard below, leaning his forehead on the cold pane. Kaylah and Chinook came around the corner of the barn, trotting together, with Bruno following. Now Chinook turned around and looked at Bruno before they began to walk slowly toward one another. Rusty paused in the doorway of the barn to watch.

Inspection time again, Scott thought. Chinook and Bruno sure have been checking each other out this past week.

"Scott,"—Caroline was standing beside him—"can I ask you something?"

"Sure, what is it?"

"Well, I was thinking about trying out for the Christmas play at school."

"Yeah?" Scott turned to look at her. She was picking at a chip of paint on the window ledge. "So what's to keep you from doing that?"

"Oh, nothing, I guess." Now she worked a chunk of paint loose. "Do you think I should?"

"I don't know. Why don't you ask Mom? Or him, why don't you ask David?" He let his voice get kind of snotty-sounding over David's name.

"Remember last year, when I played the smallest Christmas tree in the forest?"

Scott turned to look at Caroline, remembering. "Where did you get that candy bar?" he asked, watching as she unwrapped a Hershey.

"In my room," she said. "Want one?"

"Not now, before breakfast. You're gonna turn into the *fattest* Christmas tree in the forest if you don't stop eating. What's the matter with you?"

She shrugged. "I don't feel so lonesome when I eat."

"Aw, Caroline, you don't have to feel lonesome. You've got me and Mom."

"But you've got your dogs and Mom's got him."

Scott turned to the window again and looked below. She was right. He did have the dogs. Hey, what was going on down there? What were those dogs doing?

He nearly knocked Caroline down as he ran from the room.

Scott raced down the stairs, through the kitchen, and out the back door. Mom's face was a blur as he ran, and Howdy's too. No one else seemed to be around.

Then he was outside and running toward the dogs. He heard them, snarling, snapping at one another as they rolled in the snow. First Chinook was on top, then Bruno, over and over. Bodies, tails, feet, all mixed up, all snarled and snapping.

"Chinook," Scott yelled. "Come. Bruno, you too. Come here." Get control, he told himself. Do something.

But what could he do? He looked frantically around for something to throw at them, but there was only snow. In desperation he balled it up and began to pummel them, but he knew it wouldn't make a dent in Chinook's thick ruff. Tufts of fur scattered around them and drifted lazily in the air.

"Mom," Scott yelled. "Mom, bring me a broom."

Kaylah began to circle the fighting dogs now, looking as if he might join in. Rusty barked as he jumped closer and closer.

"Stay, Kaylah," Scott yelled. That's all he needed, another dog fighting. "Stop, you dumb mutts." He tried again, feeling helpless, totally useless.

Small drops of red appeared on the snow, but Scott couldn't tell who was bleeding. They kept moving, biting, snarling. Blobs of saliva dripped from their mouths.

Scott had to act. Now. Take control, that's what Mr. Wagner had said. Stay in control of the dogs. Scott couldn't let Mr. Wagner's dog get hurt because *he'd* lost control.

Suddenly Scott ran at the dogs, pounding and stamping his boots hard on the packed snow. Then he tried to grab Chinook's harness. Instantly the dogs paused to regrip and Scott felt a near-miss on his hand. Oh, lordy, were they so juiced up that they would turn on him?

"Scott, here's the broom." It was Howdy, looking scared and small.

"Get your dad, your brother, anybody," Scott yelled as he grabbed the handle.

"Brad's coming," Howdy said, staring at the dogfight. "He was still in bed, but he's coming."

Then Scott began to push the broom between the dogs, sweeping it in their faces until, gradually, the dogs began to snap at the broom instead of each other. Slowly, Scott worked the broom back and forth, back and forth, until the dogs moved away, and they stood panting, their sides heaving.

Scott watched them, waiting to see if they would begin again. Somewhere in the back of his head, he heard a door slam, then footsteps crunching in the snow.

"Bruno!" Brad yelled. "Look, he's bleeding. His paw—there's blood all over everything."

"No, there isn't," Scott said. "It just got smeary, that's all."

"That's all?" Brad turned on him, looking ready to fight too. "If it was one of your precious dogs, you'd change your tune." He took a step toward Scott, and suddenly Scott wanted to hit him, hit him hard. His fists clenched, his breath choked him, angry tears stung his eyes.

"It's all your fault," Brad yelled, coming one step closer. His face was blotchy, with pillow marks zigzagged across it.

"My fault?" Scott yelled back. "It was your dog, he attacked Chinook . . ." Not quite true, but almost. "You got a lotta nerve."

Now they were within hitting distance. Scott felt so tied up, so tense, he wondered if he could move his arms and fists if he had to. Then his heart started pumping faster and he knew. He knew all right. He could punch this guy's lights out easy.

"Your fault," Brad said so quietly that Scott knew only he could hear. Not Howdy, nor Caroline standing on the porch, watching. "Why did you have to come here?" Brad whispered. "Maybe, if you hadn't, she might have come back."

"Fat chance," Scott said hotly. "Not with you around."

Scott didn't see Brad's fist, just heard it connect on his chin with a sick, crunching sound. He staggered back, dazed, feeling white-hot pinpricks throb in his face. Then he really got mad, so damned mad . . .

He came at Brad, pummeling, pounding, not caring if he got hurt any more. He just wanted to hurt Brad, feel his fists crash into his ribs, kick him in the crotch, double him up and send him to the state of Washington with a knock-out punch.

Suddenly Scott felt a chunk of iron come down hard on his shoulder and grip it like a skip loader. Then he saw that

Brad was being held in the same vice. Neither of them could move.

Scott looked up, startled. Where had Mr. Hartfield come from? There was the jeep, its door open. He must have just driven up from somewhere. And there was Mom, standing back, hands to her mouth, tears running down her cheeks.

"Stop it, both of you." Mr. Hartfield was talking in words carved from ice. "Stop this fighting right now. I'm ashamed of both of you."

Mr. Hartfield gave each of them a shake before he released his grip on their shoulders and stepped back. "Now do something about these dogs. Take care of Bruno's foot, look at Chinook and see if he got hurt under all that fur. Do something besides think about yourselves. Why were the dogs fighting in the first place?"

Mr. Hartfield turned, almost military style, put his arms around Mom, and guided her up to the house.

"Bruno, come," Brad said, kneeling down to look at his paw. Reluctantly, Scott went over and bent down to look, too. It was a small gash and would heal quickly. Looked messy more than anything, just as he'd said.

Now Chinook and Kaylah trotted up as if nothing had happened. Dogs forget, Scott thought. But humans don't forget, ever.

A little while later it was time to go to school, and Scott moved through the morning as if he weren't there. Everything he did was automatic, nothing seemed to connect with him. The only thing he really felt was his throbbing jaw. He had to say that much for Brad, he could punch with the best of them.

Scott walked outside to the playground at noon, after skipping lunch in the cafeteria. The sun was shining, but the air had a sharp bite to it. He felt it more on his chin than anywhere else. Everywhere else he felt hot, still steaming about this morning. Brad. Man, what a jerk.

"Scott, Scott." Michelle hurried up to him, jacket open, scarf flying in the air. "Scott, do you know what Brad said in the caf? He said he's going to finish what he started this morning. He says—" She stopped and stared at his face. "Did he do that? Oh, Scott, what are you going to do?"

"Get ready. In fact, I'm ready right now."

Suddenly Scott felt calm. If Brad wanted to fight it out right here at school, that was okay with him.

Now Michelle was joined by her sister, Barbie, and Jeffrey and that other kid, Robert, who always sat with them at lunch. Usually he laughed all the time, but he wasn't laughing now.

"Scott, don't fight," Michelle was pleading. "You'll get hurt some more. I know. Brad's fought a lot here at school and he's good at it."

Scott looked down at Michelle. If only she didn't look at him like that. It made him feel so funny—weird, even. And then he remembered what Caroline had said, that Michelle was his girlfriend, and he had this secret with Brad about girls. That was funny. He didn't know enough about girls to have a secret. He just had that other secret, the one about Brad's mother.

Brad. Scott looked up, saw him walking slowly across the playground with the bunch of guys who were always hanging around him, like flies on . . .

He didn't finish the printout in his head, but he knew the word he wanted to use.

Brad was taking his own sweet time coming over here. Him and his thugs. Yeah, that's what they were. And they were trying to look so tough.

Suddenly Scott longed for Jamie at his side. He was a scrappy fighter and could quickly even these odds if it came to that.

Finally, Brad was standing about three feet away, just standing with his hands in the back pockets of his jeans, the way he always stood. His eyes were hard, the way they always looked.

"You want to finish it here?" Brad asked.

"Any place you say." Scott hoped his voice wouldn't buckle. "Just the two of us."

Then the one o'clock bell began to ring, but Scott didn't want to be the first to move, as if that would show Brad he was anxious to leave, that he was chicken. He waited, waited, waited, until finally, Brad took a step backward.

"Okay, just the two of us," Brad said. "Soon." Then he turned his back and walked slowly toward the school entrance. A moment or two later, Scott followed. He had to admit he felt relieved.

·10·

Another Upset

The sun was bright against the snow on Saturday morning, and Scott squinted as they drove along the highway to Box Elder. He wished he'd brought his goggles, the ones he wore on the trail when he was racing. But he didn't have time to look for them after Mr. Hartfield asked, at breakfast, if he would go into town with Brad and him. *Told* him to come was more like it, Scott thought. The men in the family had to have a conference, he'd said.

Mom had given Scott one of her meaningful looks across the table, so he didn't talk back nor say what was on his mind. But one of these days, look out. He'd tell Mr. Hartfield to lay lay off, stop trying so hard to be his dad.

"I suppose you boys know why I wanted to talk to you by yourselves," Mr. Hartfield was saying now. He passed a souped-up old Mustang, painted neon red.

Scott kept staring out the window, squinting against the bright snow. He'd let Brad talk first, but so far, he hadn't opened his mouth, just kept looking straight ahead. He sat in front with his dad, and Scott could keep an eye on him from the back.

"It's about what went on last Thursday morning," Mr. Hartfield said when no one answered him. "That fight you had."

Good thing he doesn't know about the one coming up, Scott thought.

"You boys have to learn to get along." Mr. Hartfield glanced in the rear-view mirror at him, but Scott looked away.

Brad sighed and scrunched further down in the front seat. He didn't like this any better than Scott did.

"So what do you say, boys?" Mr. Hartfield asked after he slowed down at the intersection with River Crossing Road. "How about deciding to be friends as well as brothers?"

Oh, man, he was really laying it on with a trowel this morning, Scott thought. Friends and brothers. Where did he get this stuff?

"Brad, I didn't hear your answer. No more fighting, okay?"

"Okay."

"And Scott?" Mr. Hartfield was looking at him in the rear-view mirror again. "It's truce time, okay?"

"Yeah."

Mr. Hartfield sighed. "Good, now let's talk about our dog team. What's been going on with them lately, Scott?"

"Well, jogging every day," Scott began. "To build up their wind and speed. Mine, too."

"How's Bruno doing?"

"He could be the third dog in harness, easy." Scott looked at the back of Brad's head. "Providing he wants to."

"No, providing I want him to." Brad turned to glare at Scott. "I haven't said you could use my dog yet."

"I'll have to know pretty soon," Scott said. "That Billings race is about three weeks away, and he's got to have some practice between Kaylah and Chinook so he knows what he's doing."

"When . . . when is that race in Billings?" Brad asked.

"The tenth of December."

"Would Bruno look good in that race?"

Scott shrugged. "Sure, if he gets enough practice. He ought to be running real nice by then."

"How about it, Brad?" Mr. Hartfield glanced at his son. "Let Scott use Bruno for his third dog. Then it would be a real family team."

"If you don't want to, that's okay," Scott said. "I can probably use Rusty or get a pickup dog from Amos." Let him keep his dumb dog.

"Well . . ." Brad paused. "Well, okay, I guess."

Finally, Scott thought, feeling tense with excitement. I've got three dogs, a team. Only two of them are Mallys, but Bruno is strong, and he'll do okay. The important thing is I can race with them and I can win. I just know it.

"Good, I'm glad that's settled," Mr. Hartfield said. "Now we're pulling together like a family. What'll we do when we get home, Scott?"

"I'm going to harness them." Scott leaned forward. "Kaylah and Chinook know what it feels like and they'll be ready, but we have to give Bruno lots of experience so he understands."

"He's smart." Brad turned around. "He'll learn fast. Is he gonna be lead dog?"

"Of course not." Scott leaned back in his seat. "Kaylah's my leader and Chinook will be wheel dog, so that leaves Bruno in the middle."

"Nobody can see him if he's in the middle."

"Everybody can see him there just fine." Scott tried not to sound impatient.

"Yeah, Brad, I don't know what you're so worried about," Mr. Hartfield said.

I do, Scott thought. He wants to impress his mom with

my team, so that means he's gonna invite her to the meet. Wonder how Mr. Hartfield will like that?

Fifteen minutes later, they pulled up in front of the feed store.

"You boys want to come inside with me?" Mr. Hartfield opened his door. "I'm just going to get some vitamin pellets for the horses."

"I've got stuff of my own to do," Brad said. He opened the car door on his side.

"I'll stay here." Scott felt impatient now, eager to be back at the farm, working the dogs.

"Okay. Be back in a few minutes." Mr. Hartfield stepped out of the car and walked up the steps to the Feed and Seed.

Brad walked down the street to the post office. Another letter to his mom, Scott thought. I wonder if she ever writes back.

Then Scott began to watch the Saturday morning crowd hurry along the walk. He recognized a couple of kids from school who looked as if they were cruising, without any special place to go. Then his math teacher stepped out of the store, carrying a sack of chicken feed. Was everyone in this town a farmer? Scott wondered.

Suddenly he sat up straight. Look who was coming down the street, taking giant strides, towering above everyone else. Scott opened the car door and jumped out.

"Amos," he yelled. "Amos, wait a minute. Remember me?"

The big man looked over, then covered the space between them in two steps. "Hey, it's my musher friend," he said, crushing Scott's hand in his paw. "Did you get my notice about the race in a few weeks?"

"Sure did," Scott answered. "Do you live around here?"

"No, I live down in Billings, but I call on the feed store every two or three weeks. I'm a grain salesman for this part of the state. Tell me, how's that beautiful Mally of yours? Did you get a team put together yet?"

"Today, just today. And I'm gonna race in Billings." Scott said.

"That's great."

Then Scott began to tell him about Chinook and Bruno and his plans to put them together in harness with Kaylah this afternoon.

"I don't suppose you can come out and watch or anything, can you?" Scott asked.

"I sure would like to, but I've got to get on the road for home. I'm glad I ran into you, though. There's going to be a workout next Friday, the day after Thanksgiving, at the Hellan ranch. It's just south of town here, and you ought to try your dogs in it. Should be good experience for them, expecially the new dog."

"I'll remember that," Scott said. "Next Friday at the Hellans'."

"See you then," Amos said.

Scott climbed back into the car and watched Amos's big frame grow smaller as he hurried down the block.

A few minutes later Mr. Hartfield and Brad came back.

"Guess who I just saw." Scott couldn't hold the words back.

"Santa Claus," Brad said.

"He had the beard for it," Scott answered. Then quickly he filled them in on his talk with Amos.

Mr. Hartfield eased the car out of its parking spot before he said, "you boys have a lot of work to do before then."

The ten mile ride back to the ranch seemed to take forever by Scott's reckoning. Finally, they turned into their long driveway.

"Aren't you going to stop?" Brad asked.

"It's too early for the mailman."

"Maybe he changed his route."

"Okay, okay." Mr. Hartfield stopped the car, and Brad ran across to the mailbox.

"Brad must have entered a contest the way he keeps looking for mail," Mr. Hartfield said.

Scott avoided looking in the rear-view mirror. He wants me to tell him what I know, Scott thought. But he needs to ask Brad, not me. Why doesn't he act more like a dad to his own kid?

Brad didn't say anything when he climbed back into the car. He didn't have to. His face said it all.

Scott didn't go inside the house when they stopped in the barnyard. Instead, he hurried into the barn, grabbed the harnesses and the sled. After checking the equipment to make sure he had everything, Scott pushed the sled outdoors.

Kaylah and Chinook hurried over for a look.

"Today's the day," he said to them. His mouth felt dry and he swallowed his excitement.

Then Scott knelt down beside the sled, letting his thumbs get in the way of his fingers as he tried to fasten the towline. Why couldn't he get it right? He'd done it a thousand times before.

A pickup truck turned into their drive at the blacktop, but it was too far away to recognize the people inside.

Then the back door slammed, and Howdy and Caroline crunched across the snowy barnyard toward him. "Mom said don't start until she takes your picture," Caroline said.

"I'm going to take your picture, too," Howdy said. "Your mom's been showing me how to use a camera."

"She never showed me how," Caroline said.

"Maybe you never asked her," Brad said, giving her cap a yank.

Scott looked up, startled. "Pick on somebody your own size."

"Okay, I will." Brad kicked up some snow with his boots. "Are you sure you know what you're doing?"

Scott attached Kaylah's harness to a tugline, running it over the dog's hips to the towline already fastened to the sled. Then he answered slowly, "Sure. You might even learn something if you watch. Bruno's next. Grab him, will you?"

"There's only one reason I'm doing this," Brad said. He grabbed Bruno and gave him a quick hug.

"How do you know she'll even come to the meet?" Scott asked.

"Who?" Caroline asked.

"Both of you McClures ask too many questions." Brad glared at them before he turned away, scattering snow in a riff behind his boots and heading for the porch.

"I wish I knew what was the matter with Brad," Howdy said, staring after him. "He isn't much fun any more."

"Was he ever?" Caroline asked.

"Yeah. For a brother, he used to be a lot of fun. He talked to me a lot without being snarly all the time."

Like the time we rode up toward the Bearpaws, Scott thought. He was decent then, almost normal.

Scott tuned out Howdy and Caroline as he grabbed Bruno's collar. Then he placed the harness on the dog and attached it to the towline. Bruno shook himself and looked around at the tugline on his hips.

"I may have to get some sheepskin and make some pads for him." Scott said, looking up at Howdy and Caroline. "He's not quite as big as the dog who used to wear this harness."

"Now what?" Howdy asked.

"Now I do the same thing with Chinook that I did with Kaylah and Bruno." Scott began to fit Chinook's big body with his harness and tugline. "He's my wheel dog."

"Wheel dog?" Howdy said. "I don't see any wheels."

"Of course not, dummy," Caroline said. "It just means he's the one right in front of the sled."

"How am I supposed to know that?" Howdy looked cross. It must be everyone's day for it. But not Scott's. Not today.

He stood up and pulled on his mittens and looked at each snaphook before he spoke. "Well, this is it." Scott couldn't believe it. He was going to take his team out on its first run. His team. His very own team. His insides were bubbly, like a glass of soda.

"Whose pickup is that?" Howdy asked.

Scott glanced at the truck pulling to a stop near the house. It looked familiar. He'd seen it before. Mr. Hartfield and Mom were just coming outside and they waved and smiled. Oh, no . . .

"Guess who?" Brad called in his best syrupy voice.

It was Michelle and her dad and little sister. What were they doing here? "You didn't . . ." Scott looked accusingly at Brad.

"Not me," he protested. "I'm innocent. I didn't know she was coming."

Scott decided not to wait, just go ahead and run the dogs. He couldn't stand all the drippy looks from Michelle right now, especially in front of Brad.

Scott kicked the sled's steel-claw brake loose from the

snow, stepped on the runners, grabbed the handlebar, and leaned forward. He wasn't going to ride yet; the dogs weren't ready to carry his weight so soon. But he just had to get the feel of it before he started.

Then Mom yelled. "Scott, wait, don't go. Don't go. I want to take your picture."

But it was too late. Kaylah heard one word, go, and that's what he did. The sled lurched forward, picking up speed.

Scott slipped, off balance, from the runners, and was dumped on his back in the hard-packed snow. It nearly knocked the breath from him, and he only managed to wheeze out, "Stop them, stop the dogs."

Brad stared openmouthed after the running dogs while Scott struggled to get to his feet. Behind him, Scott could hear Howdy yelling, "Go, go, go."

Dumb idiot, Scott thought, running after the dogs and sled. "Shut up. Be quiet," he yelled.

Now Brad began to chase the dogs, too; then Mr. Hartfield and Michelle's dad, and even Michelle joined in. Little by little, Bruno's awkwardness slowed Kaylah's momentum until Scott could reach out and grab the sled, bringing them to a stop.

Scott rested his head on the handlebar, breathing hard in great gulps and wanting to crawl under a snowdrift and not come out to face anyone until the spring thaw. He felt so utterly stupid.

"Wow, that was some race," Brad said, hurrying up to him. "Except, I thought dogs always ran against other dogs, not their drivers."

He began to laugh and so did Howdy. Even Caroline. And then he heard her high-pitched giggle, too. Even Michelle was laughing at him now.

·11·

Letting Go

Scott walked slowly up the driveway on Wednesday afternoon after school, watching Caroline and Howdy walk ahead of him. He didn't know where Brad was. He'd gotten off the bus but had stopped to talk to some kids who lived down the road. He must have gone home with them.

Rusty was posing by the back-porch steps for Mom's camera when Scott rounded the corner of the house. "Straighten your tie, Rusty," Scott called. "Mom's taking all these pictures so you can get a job in the movies." Scott couldn't resist the dig and smiled as Mom turned around. When she got on a project, she was like a Mally pup with a dishrag. She wouldn't let go for love or money.

"This is the last one I'm going to send in to the newspaper." Mom put the cover on her lens, then brushed her dark hair away from her forehead. "But I couldn't resist one more. Look at him. Rusty is actually chubby now and his coat is so shiny you can see yourself in it. And he feels so good he's actually smiling."

Scott looked at Rusty. He did seem to have a smile on his face. "Yeah, you're right. His owners will recognize him for sure now. This is the way he must have looked before he got shot."

"That's why I decided to try one more snap," Mom said. "The only trouble is . . ."

"What?"

"I don't know what I'm going to do if someone claims him." Mom's voice was quiet. "I like that sweet mutt."

"Yeah," Scott answered after a moment. "Me, too."

"It's hard, isn't it, Scott?"

Scott thought about her question, wondering. "What, Mom?"

"Letting go."

Scott looked at her. Did she really mean letting go of Rusty? Not totally. No, she must know what he was feeling about tomorrow, their first Thanksgiving without Dad. But how? Not because she was having problems. After all, she got married again right away.

"Do you ever think about Dad?" Scott asked. He drew lines in the slushy snow with the toe of his boot.

"Of course I do, and I'll never forget him." Mom took a couple of steps toward Scott and reached out her hand to touch the sleeve of his jacket. "He'll always be a part of me and who I am. But I've learned that it's okay to make room for other people in my life. It's okay to love others."

Scott looked at Mom's hand on his sleeve. Her fingers were long and tapered like white candles with soft pink color on her nails that glowed against the dark blue of his jacket.

He listened to her words echo inside his head, felt them bounce around and around, looking for a place to land. Finally, they settled into a waiting place until he could think about them and come to terms with their meaning.

The back door opened and Caroline stomped out on the porch. "Your girlfriend is on the telephone and wants to talk to you."

Scott's face felt as if it had caught on fire. "Tell her I'm not home."

"Scott." Mom sounded disappointed. "Why don't you talk to Michelle? She really likes you, wants to be your friend."

"Well, I'm not sure, especially after last Saturday when she . . . when they laughed."

"Scott, be a good sport about it." Mom's voice sounded crisp. "You can take a little teasing."

"Certain people who dish it out should learn to take some, too."

"You're being too hard on Brad. He's such a troubled boy, Scott."

"He's trouble, all right."

"That's not what I meant and you know it." Mom reached down to pat Rusty. "Now go inside and make your peace with Michelle and . . . by the way, where's Brad?"

"Search me." Scott slowly walked up to the porch. Okay, so he'd talk to Michelle and Brad, but he was going to show them what he could do, come Saturday. He'd score such good times at the practice meet that every other team on the course would eat his snow.

Caroline stood beside the open back door. "Scott's got a girlfriend," she whispered.

"Stow it, creepy," he answered back.

He walked into the hallway and picked up the telephone. "Hi, Michelle. There's gonna be a practice meet on Saturday at the Hellans'. Do you want to come?"

He waited while she went into orbit. "Oh, Scott. You're actually inviting me? Oh, this is so neat. I was just calling about it because Susie Hellan told me and so I thought . . . can I help? Can I feed the dogs or brush them or whatever you do to get ready?"

"No, Brad is supposed to be my handler, providing he

shows up. If he doesn't, then his dad will do it." Scott sighed, wishing he had someone with more experience to back him up. Come to think of it, he wished he had more experience, too, and someone like Amos or Mr. Wagner as his second man. Oh, well, if he used his head, what could go wrong?

"See you Saturday," Michelle was saying.

"Okay. Bye."

"Scott. Happy Thanksgiving tomorrow."

"Oh, sure. You, too."

The next morning Scott got up early and took the dogs for a long run. He returned just in time to see Mom lift a blue roasting pan from the oven. Now he waited while she took the lid from the roaster to reveal the shiny, brown turkey inside. Steam and scent rose together as Scott took a pinch of hot dressing that spilled from the bird.

"You'll burn your tongue," Mom yelled.

"It's worth it," Scott said as he hurried into the hall and up the stairs.

By the time he'd washed and dressed, dinner was nearly ready. He glanced into the dining room where a fire crackled busily in the fireplace. Six green candles marched down the center of the thick, white cloth on the table. Pinecones and dried birch leaves were scattered in between.

"Want me to light the candles, Mom?" Scott called into the kitchen.

"Not yet, but put the chairs around, please. Get Brad to help." Scott did it himself. He smiled as he stepped around Mom's camera fastened to a tripod. They couldn't escape her lens even for one day.

"Here we are," Mom said, hurrying in, carrying bowls of food. Mr. Hartfield followed, carrying the turkey. Howdy and Caroline followed him, each carrying more food.

"Where's Brad?" Mr. Hartfield asked, putting the turkey down in front of his place.

"He was up in his room a little while ago," Howdy said. "I'll call him." He walked out into the hall.

"You sit there, Caroline," Mom said. "And you, there, Scott." Her voice was quivery, her cheeks pink, and her eyes looked shiny. "Over there, Howdy. As soon as Brad comes, I want to take a picture."

"Aren't you going to be in it, Margaret?" Mr. Hartfield asked.

"Oh, yes. I've got a timer," Mom answered.

"Good, then it will be a real family picture."

They exchanged a look that Scott added to his lovey-dovey collection.

Brad's footsteps on the stairs were slow and deliberate. Mr. Hartfield pinched his lips together, but Mom shook her head. "Right there, Brad," she said, pointing to a chair when he entered the room. "Hold still a sec." Mom peered into the camera, adjusted it, then turned on the timer and ran to stand beside Mr. Hartfield. "Say cheese, please," she laughed.

The camera clicked, and the strobe flashed at the same instant.

"Now let's eat," Howdy said.

"Wait until we light the candles." Mom handed matches around. "One candle for each member of the family."

One by one they lit a candle. Scott felt each person thinking deep, private thoughts as he did now, watching the dancing flames cast shadows on the flowery wallpaper.

"That was nice, Margaret," Mr. Hartfield said.

"Yeah, nice," Howdy echoed. "Now please pass the potatoes."

Everyone laughed. Even Brad cracked a smile as the bowl of mashed potatoes was passed to Howdy. Other bowls of food circled the table—apple and raisin stuffing, sweet potatoes with walnuts, cranberry salad, peas, and creamed green beans, Scott's very favorite. Mom hadn't forgotten. Today, he'd eat a ton of everything after his workout this morning. And he had to store up extra carbs for the meet day after tomorrow. Extra carbs meant extra strength, Dad used to say.

Mr. Hartfield dealt out slabs of white and dark meat to everyone, then Mom passed the gravy boat to Howdy. He looked as if he'd died and gone to heaven.

A comfortable silence settled over the table as they began to eat. The warmth of the fire, the brightness of the candles, the taste of the food covered them all like a soft, warm blanket. Scott felt its presence, felt himself dipping into the comfort and actually enjoying it. He hadn't meant to, knew he wasn't ready, but it was happening anyway. How can I feel like this? he wondered. How can I feel like this without Dad?

"I think I need more gravy." Howdy arranged his peas carefully.

"Here it is," Mom said.

"Thanks, Mom," Howdy answered.

"You're welcome, son," Mom said.

Scott looked up to see Brad staring at Mom and Howdy, his mouth a pencil slash across his face. Handle it, Brad, Scott thought, trying to send him a messsage. Don't you think it's hard for me, too?

Scott looked at Mom, tears glistening in her eyes as she watched Howdy eat. She's made room, Scott thought. She's made room for him and now I've got to do it, too. Make room for all of them, even Brad. At least, I've got to try.

But judging from the look on Brad's face, he wasn't buying any of this family stuff.

Scott woke early on Saturday morning, tense and eager for the practice run to begin in a few hours. He jumped out of bed to look at the snow. Good, nothing had changed from yesterday. It was glistening with crystals on its hard crust. The snow would be fast today. Maybe an all-time-best fast.

He threw on his clothes and raced downstairs.

After breakfast everyone pitched in to help with the dogs and the sled and the equipment they'd need for the race. Then they all piled in the station wagon. Scott sat in back with the three dogs while everyone else sat in front.

"Are you sure you cinched the rope tight enough on the sled?" Mr. Hartfield asked, looking in the rear-view mirror at Scott. "I'd hate to have the sled sail off the top of the car while we're out on the highway."

"I'm sure," Scott answered.

"Everybody ready?" Mr. Hartfield asked.

"Wait a sec," Mom said. "Look at Rusty, sitting there by the steps. Can't we bring him, too?"

He did look pretty lonesome, Scott thought. "I'll get him, Mom." Scott jumped out of the car, whistling. Rusty loped over to him and leaped into the open end of the station wagon.

"Got room, Scott?" Mom asked.

"Just barely." He laughed as Kaylah and Rusty ganged up to wash his face.

It wasn't far to the Hellan ranch, three miles down the highway, then two miles east on Lake Elmo Road. Scott felt his excitement build as they turned into the driveway.

They pulled into the barnyard and parked near other wagons and pickups. Dogs were chained to stake-out leashes, barking and chattering to one another. I'm not the only excited one here today, Scott thought.

He hopped out of the car, and before the dogs could jump out, Scott grabbed their leashes to hold them steady until Brad came around to help.

"Now what?" Brad asked. "Just stake them out and wait our turn?"

"That's about it," Scott said. You can straighten the harnesses if you want while I see what position I've drawn."

He had spotted Amos the moment he looked up from the dogs, and now he pushed his way past other people and equipment toward the big man.

"Scott, I've been looking for you." Amos thumbed through a stack of numbered tags. "Here's your position and it looks like you've got a good one. Have a good run today."

"Thanks." Scott hesitated. "Can you tell me something about the trail?"

"Let's see." Amos scratched his beard and looked out to the meadow. "Nothing special. Oh, yes, there's a narrow, winding part by the creek bed just before you enter the final stretch. We put that in to test your coordination."

"Thanks." Scott grinned at him. "Just what I needed."

When he got back to Brad and the dogs, Michelle was there, pacing back and forth in the snow.

"I'm so wired," she said. "This is so exciting I just can't stand it."

"Turn around everyone," Mom called.

"Oh, Mom, not another picture," Scott groaned.

"There, see how painless that was?" Mom rolled her film forward and went back to the car.

Then Scott began to examine the sled, checking the lines, the joints tied with rawhide leather, and especially the steel-claw brake.

"How does it look, Scott?" Mr. Hartfield was beside him now.

"Everything checks out fine. The dogs are okay, too. Now all I have to do is get a good workout time."

"You will, don't worry. You'll be the best today."

I hope, Scott thought, watching Mr. Hartfield go over and talk to Brad.

Half an hour later, the dogs were in harness, with Kaylah leading, then Bruno, and then Chinook as wheel dog. Scott guided the dogs into position and waited. It seemed forever before Amos motioned him forward.

"The trail is a little icy, so be careful going around that first turn," Amos said, watching the team that had pulled out ahead of Scott.

"Okay." Scott felt a trickle of sweat slip down his back. Was he that hot? No, just nervous. Man, was he nervous!

"Next up," Amos called and looked at Scott.

Scott guided the dogs to the starting line and watched the flagman. "Ready," he whispered to the dogs and felt a quiver that traveled like an electric current through the reins into his mittens. The dogs were snapped taut in their traces; even Bruno had the fever now. Scott stood on his sled runners, and for one brief second, everything was quiet under the big sky. He could feel everyone's eyes on him, waiting, waiting.

"It's a go," the flagman yelled, bringing his flag down to the ground.

The dogs were off and Scott leaped from the runners to pump them quickly into a hard, driving rhythm. "Go," he yelled. "Go, dogs, go." Their ears laid flat against their heads, their tongues flapped as they ran.

Kaylah was into a full lope and Scott knew they couldn't keep this pace for the entire distance or they would wear themselves out. But, for now, he let them run, and he ran, too, finally jumping on the runners as the trail wound downhill into a meadow that was cut wide and deep and long.

Scott watched the red flags that marked the edge of the trail and kept well to the middle where the snow was packed down by other teams who'd run before them. Now Kaylah slowed and settled into a trot that wouldn't tire them before the workout was finished. Good dog.

"Haw," Scott called as the trail swung sharply left. They responded quickly, and even Bruno seemed to understand the need for it.

Trail spotters waved to him from their positions as Scott flashed his biggest smile. He knew he was running his all-time best today, could feel it with every creak of the sled. He just couldn't stop grinning. The grin stayed on his face; maybe it was frozen there. If only Jamie were here to see this run.

The trail swung sharply right now and the team took the turn easily. No problems, everything was A-OK. Scott glanced off to the right, to the wood beyond. This was some gorgeous spread. About the best-looking ranch he'd seen. In summer, it must be as . . .

"Look out ahead."

He heard the voice, snapped his head back to the trail, feeling a stab of anticipation grab his chest. Must be the narrow part coming up, the part Amos said . . .

It was worse. A runaway team was coming straight at him. "Runaway team," he yelled, hoping a spotter would hear. "Runaway."

No time to yell any more, decide now, decide what to do. "Whoa," he called. "Halt, stop." They slowed as Scott looked right, then left. The trail was so narrow he couldn't manuever, and neither could the other team. Closer and closer, the other dogs weren't even slowing down. "Stop," he yelled at them. "Whoa."

Kaylah stopped, but the other team was nearly on them, running full out. Then Scott was running, too, grabbing Kaylah, pulling him off the trail, hoping Bruno would get the idea. Chinook would know, but Bruno? Oh, come on, Bruno.

They fell down the side of the trail toward the creek bed, over and over in a tangle of legs and harness and lines and sled. Then it was still as Scott lay in the snow, waiting for his head to clear.

"Team down," someone yelled from a faraway place.

"You okay?" another voice called. Then squeaky footsteps in the snow. "Hey, I'm sorry. Jeez, I'm sorry."

Scott stood up and realized he was all right. Kaylah stood up and shook himself. Now Chinook did, too.

"Looks like your team is okay. Oh, man, this could have

been a total disaster if the teams had collided. Thanks for what you did."

"I was having my all-time best today." Scott stared at the guy, hating him. He was big, maybe sixteen, but Scott was mad enough to take him on anyway.

"I don't know how it happened." The guy began to right the sled. "I don't know what else to say. Oh, no."

Scott whirled around and looked down. "Bruno," he said. "Bruno, get up, boy. Come on." But he wasn't moving. Bruno wasn't moving at all.

·12·

Why Did It Happen?

Quickly Scott freed Bruno from the sled. Then he moved it, leaving Kaylah and Chinook still attached so they wouldn't wander away. He didn't know what to do next; whether to touch Bruno, to feel for broken bones, or to look for a terrible bruise that made him stay so quiet, so still. He was afraid to touch him for fear he'd hurt the dog more. Scott knew, deep down inside, that he'd caused this. He'd wanted to race so much that he'd talked Brad into using his dog when he might not have been ready. It's all my fault, Scott thought. I did it. I'll never race again.

Then Scott heard the roar of a snowmobile, and a couple of men rushed up. One of them was Doc Hansen, the vet who'd worked on Rusty. How had he gotten here so fast? Sure, the spotters. They must have radioed in to the starting line.

"Let me look," Doc Hansen said. He knelt down and began to touch with careful, knowing fingers.

A vet, here at this practice meet? It wasn't a sanctioned race, so how come Doc was here? Then Scott remembered Amos. He'd organized it, he was responsible, and he would never leave anything to chance. Especially a dog's life. Not like certain other people. Not like me, Scott thought.

"Is he gonna be okay?" The kid, whose team had run

away, asked. "Oh, man, I sure hope so. I feel so awful, it's all my fault."

"No, it isn't," Scott said, quiet-like, under his breath. "Go get your dogs and take them in. Tell . . . tell . . . no, never mind. I'll tell when I get there." He had to tell Brad himself.

"Hey, I'm really sorry," the kid said again. Then he walked to his own dogs who had slowed down and now doubled back on the trail toward them. They looked beat. They'd stretched out, used all their energy on their run-away. Scott hoped they could get back to the starting line.

Doc Hansen and the other man worked on Bruno until Scott couldn't watch any more. It hurt, cut like a serrated blade scratching on his insides. So he went over to Kaylah and Chinook who waited patiently, sitting in the snow beside the sled.

"It's all right, Kaylah," Scott said, ruffing his fur and staring into his dark, almond-shaped eyes. The dog stood up and leaned against Scott's legs, as if trying to communicate his understanding. Now Chinook got up and stood close, too. They were so warm, as they tried to love Scott with their closeness, that he wanted to bawl. It was all he could do to keep his hurt from spilling out of his eyes. As it was, Scott's nose began to drip, just like a little kid's, and he had to wipe it with his mitten. Me, wiping, at my age, Scott thought. He knelt down and buried himself in the dogs' fur that was tingly-cold with snow, felt their bodies move rhythmically while they panted out of sync with one another.

"Scott."

He looked up to see Amos, tall as a redwood against the bright blue sky. "I did it." Scott began to blubber. "I killed Bruno."

Amos grabbed Scott by one arm and stood him up on his feet, almost planted him there, hard and kind of brusque. It jarred Scott so much that he could feel it in the fillings in his teeth.

"Stop it," Amos said. "You did what any experienced driver would have done. You saved a lot of dogs from being hurt or even killed."

"But not Brad's," Scott said. "Not Brad's. If I hadn't insisted, Bruno wouldn't have raced and he'd be alive right now."

"That kind of talk doesn't help anyone, especially you." Amos brushed snow off Scott's jacket. "And Bruno isn't dead. He's still alive, so there's hope for him. Use your energy to do something now, this minute, instead of worrying about what's already happened. Did you bring a dog bag?"

Of course. Why hadn't Scott thought to get it out and give it to Doc right away? Every driver carried a nylon bag on his sled in case a dog developed sore feet and had to ride home. Quickly Scott found his and held it out to Amos.

"No," he said. His voice was unbending, like an icicle. "You take it to Bruno. He still needs you."

Scott walked back to where Bruno lay, trying not to look, but having to, anyway. Amos said Bruno was still alive, but where? Where was the alive part of him? Was it a small spark inside, deep down, waiting to be warmed again, breathed back to life? The vet wouldn't have any magic for that.

Suddenly Scott knelt down. "Bruno," he said. "Bruno, stay. Stay."

"He's not going anywhere," someone said. "Not in the shape he's in."

Scott didn't bother to explain that wasn't what he meant. He didn't give the dog a command to stay in one spot, not moving. He just wanted Bruno to stay here in this world. Scott had to do that much for Brad. And for himself, too. Now, for the first time, this dog was family.

Doc carefully wrapped Bruno in the dog bag, put him even more carefully in the snowmobile and then they were gone, snow spraying up a curtain over their leaving.

Amos and the other man who'd come on the snowmobile began to walk toward a collection of pickups and station wagons that looked like kiddie cars in the distance. Another sled-dog team drove by so the practice meet was still going on. It seemed like forever to Scott since it had begun.

Scott drove Kaylah and Chinook back to the starting place. He drove them slowly because he knew they were tired and because he was dreading the moment when he'd have to face Brad. But when he got back, Brad had gone with Doc to his clinic in Box Elder.

Quickly, not talking much, Scott and the others packed up Kaylah and Chinook and the sled in the car. Rusty sat quietly beside him on the way home, wanting to love Scott whenever he was asked.

Later that night, Scott rode into town with Mr. Hartfield to pick up Brad at Doc's. Doc wouldn't say anything one way or the other about Bruno's chances, and Brad wouldn't say anything at all. Not even when they got home and went inside where Mom had hot cocoa waiting. He didn't even say no, he didn't want any. He just went upstairs to his room and closed the door.

By Monday, Brad had finally started to talk. Little things like yes and no, sometimes even to Scott. And Bruno was still alive, attached to one of those IV things after an operation, but still alive and wagging his tail, Brad said. Yes, he'd said that much. And Scott could feel a lot more words bottled up inside the guy, waiting, just waiting to be said.

At the bus stop after school on Monday, Brad said more, "I'm going to the vet's. I'll get home by myself."

"I'll go with you," Scott said.

"Me, too," Howdy spoke up. "I want to go."

"No, only I can visit," Brad said. "Doc said only I can go in and see Bruno."

"Never heard of that in an animal hospital," Caroline said. "Besides, we all love Bruno, so why can't we visit?"

"You two go on home." Scott gave her the beginning of a push. "Tell Mom I'm staying with Brad."

Howdy and Caroline didn't like it much, but finally, they got on the bus. Brad and Scott watched as it pulled out of the school grounds.

"Don't get the idea you're staying on my account," Brad said.

"We ought to talk pretty soon," Scott began.

"We don't have anything to talk about."

"Yes, we do." Scott tried to get Brad to look at him.

"Later," Brad said. "Later, we have a lot of unfinished business to settle up." He let his eyes meet Scott's for a flicker of a glance, then he looked away. "Now, I've got to see Bruno."

Scott watched him walk down the block, toward town, knowing what Brad meant. They still had a fight hanging in the air between them. And Bruno, too. He was afraid to think of what might happen between them if Bruno died. Come to think of it though, it couldn't be much worse than it was right now.

"Scott, where are you going?" Michelle began to walk beside him.

"Oh, hi, Michelle." He shifted his book bag to a better position. "I . . . I missed the bus."

"We'll take you home, if you don't mind going down to J. C. Penney's first. Mom had some errands in town and said to meet her there."

Scott's feelings gave him different signals now. He was glad not to have to call Mom and ask her to drive all the way in, but he suddenly felt so self-conscious being alone with Michelle like this. If any of the guys in their class saw them walking together, headed for town, they might think they liked each other in that special way. Someone might even think they were having a date.

"Where's your sister?" Scott demanded.

"She went over to a friend's house. Come on, maybe we'll have time for a Coke before we meet Mom."

So he went, wondering how something could get so out of control that he didn't know how to handle it. Lots of things, really. The accident on Saturday, being here with Michelle, and before, coming to Montana in the first place had all unleashed emotions Scott never knew he owned. Now what was he supposed to do with them? Maybe he'd know when he grew up, but until then, what could he do? Why hadn't someone told him that growing up wasn't for sissies?

"I'm totally amazed that you missed the bus," Michelle said after a moment. "I figured you'd beat it on home to work with your dogs for the race in Billings."

"I'm not gonna race them," Scott said. "Not now."

"Scott McClure." Michelle stopped in the middle of the sidewalk, forcing Scott to stop, too. "You can't quit now."

He stared at her, stared into her light blue eyes, noticing the sprinkle of freckles that scattered across her cheeks. Funny, he'd never noticed them before. He had the awful, terrible urge to reach out and touch them.

Scott turned and began to hurry down the street, his breath caught somewhere between his stomach and his shoelaces.

"Scott, did you hear me?" Michelle was running after him. "Can't you use Rusty in Bruno's place?"

"What if the same thing happened to Rusty that happened to Bruno? Besides, he's not ready." Scott walked faster, practically ran.

"That's a lie," Michelle yelled. "He's been running with you and the other dogs. You said yourself he was in good shape. All you have to do is put a harness on him and . . ."

"Well, I'm not gonna do it." He stopped and whirled around to look at her.

"You are the most stubborn, mule-headed, pig-brained boy I've ever met in all my life." Michelle was really flaming. He'd never seen her like this. "Give me one good reason why you aren't going to race."

They stood there, toe to toe, practically nose to nose, while Scott fought down everything he'd been feeling since Dad died. All the hopes, the dreams, but mostly the other thing he only let surface at night, when he could be alone and not let anyone know. His mouth began to move, there was an earthquake inside him, it was all coming to the surface, out of his mouth. He couldn't stop it.

"I'm afraid," he whispered. "It might happen again."

Michelle stared at him and he stared back. Then her mouth began to move, too. "Welcome to the club," she whispered back.

Michelle, afraid? Sure, girls were supposed to be scared

of snakes and mice and the dark. But he wasn't talking about that. He was talking heavy-duty stuff when you got scared because someone died and you thought you were the only one in the world it happened to. And worse. It could happen again.

"Sure, I get scared a lot, but I try not to let it show," she said softly. "I want to be popular—you know, one of the in-group. But I'm not, and it's scary to think I don't have what it takes and maybe I never will."

"But I like you," Scott blurted out. Then he realized what he'd said and felt his face turn into a Roman candle.

Michelle grinned. "Mom said there'd be special people who'd come along and like me and make up for all the kids who think I'm a nerd."

"Your mom?" Scott asked. "You talked to your mom about being afraid?"

"I know it sounds weird, but I talk to her a lot. She says everybody is afraid sometime during their lives. Even grown-ups. Even heroes. And she says it's okay as long as you don't let it take over everything else."

That's what I'm doing now, Scott thought. Letting it take over. But it doesn't have to be that way.

They didn't talk the rest of the way to Penney's. But Scott did a lot of thinking, especially about what Michelle's mom said. And finally he did some deciding. Making up his mind. It hadn't been that hard when you got down to it, but it sure helped to have Michelle to talk to.

They found Michelle's mom trying on shoes. "Hi," she said. "Do you kids want to stop for malteds before we go home?"

"I'm in kind of a hurry," Scott said. "I still have to run my dogs this afternoon."

"And I shouldn't be drinking malts either." Mrs. Weaver

smiled as she put her own shoes on now. "Not with my heifer hips."

They walked out of the store and down Main Street to their pickup. "Michelle told me what happened last Saturday," Mrs. Weaver said as they pulled out to the highway. "I'm glad you haven't let it stop you. From what I understand, you did a brave thing to keep those teams from colliding."

Scott nodded as he thought ahead to the race in Billings. Rusty could substitute easily for Bruno. Maybe he wouldn't run as fast or be as strong. They probably wouldn't win, maybe wouldn't even place. But he and his dogs would run and that was the important thing. They would not be afraid to try it again.

Michelle was the first to notice the strange car parked in the barnyard.

"Looks like you've got company, Scott," she said.

"Wonder who it is?" he said, hoping someone from Truckee had come for a visit. "Thanks for the ride."

"See you tomorrow," Michelle called as they turned around and headed for the hard road.

Scott hurried inside to the kitchen. A man and a woman, kind of wrinkled and bent, sat at the kitchen table with Mom.

"Here he is," Mom said, turning to look at him. Her eyes seemed kind of glittery, as if she wanted to cry, but wouldn't. He'd seen that look a lot, but not since they moved to Montana.

Now the man stood up and walked over to Scott. "I just wanted to thank you for taking such good care of our dog."

Scott's head was scrambling, trying to take hold of what was happening. "Your dog?" he finally asked.

"Yes. I understand you call him Rusty. We call him Cameron."

"Rusty?" Scott shook his head.

"We saw the picture your mother took for the newspaper. The last one, she said." Now the woman was speaking quietly. "We've been away and didn't know that Cameron had been lost and hurt. The people who were taking care of him were careless, let him out of a fenced yard."

"But we're grateful to you, young man." The man took over again, holding out some money to Scott. He just stared at it, refusing to touch it. How could this be happening?

•13•

A Hard Time With Waiting

Scott still couldn't believe it three days later. He couldn't believe that Rusty's owners would show up, just when he had decided to put him in harness for the big race in Billings. Just when everything depended on Rusty, he was taken away. Even more than that, Scott missed him. Missed that sweet, gentle creature who loved the farm, loved the other dogs, loved each member of the family unconditionally. He even loved Brad.

Scott threw his jacket on early Thursday morning, slipped out of the house, and hurried across the barnyard to feed Kaylah and Chinook. He had to decide what he was going to do about Billings. There was only one week left. Maybe he'd call Amos to see if he could borrow a dog, or maybe . . . maybe he'd just forget it. What was he trying to prove anyway? What was the point? Why not forget it? Let Chinook and Kaylah get fat and lazy. And he, Scott, would just get . . . older. Older, without having tried. Was that what he wanted?

The light was on in the barn. "Hello," Scott called out. "Anyone here?" Mr. Hartfield would have a fit if someone left the light on when it wasn't needed.

Brad stepped out of Georgia O'Keefe's stall, a curry brush in one hand. "Did you think your dogs turned the light on?" he asked.

"Maybe. They're pretty smart," Scott snapped back. "So what are you doing out here so early?"

"Haven't paid much attention to Georgia the last couple of days," he said. "Thought I'd better get her spruced up."

"Are you planning to take her to Billings?"

"Maybe not right away." Brad flipped the curry brush over and over in his hands. "Might have to wait until I see where we'll be living and all."

"Might want to see if your mom has room for Georgia . . . or anybody else."

"She's got room for me." Brad's eyes flared with anger. "Before she left here, she told me to come any time. Any time at all. And bring Bruno, too, she said."

"But that was a couple of years ago," Scott reminded him. "What's she said lately?"

"Everything's cool." Brad dropped the brush and kicked it hard. "Besides, it's none of your business, is it?"

"And I'm not losing any sleep over it either," Scott said. "But why don't you tell your dad, huh? It seems to me you owe him that much."

"I'll tell my dad when I'm good and ready." Brad went back inside the stall to Georgia. Scott picked up the curry brush and gave it a toss inside before he opened the gate for the dogs.

Kaylah and Chinook stood up and stretched as he walked into the stall. They waited for their morning hello and pat before they went outside. Then Scott began to fill their pans with kibble.

Brad suddenly appeared in the doorway. "What are you

going to do about the race in Billings if you don't have three dogs? You're still going, aren't you?"

"I don't know," Scott said. "I could race in the two-dog event, but it's mostly for beginners and babies. I'm not sure I'd be allowed in it."

"Because you're such a super sledder, you mean?" Brad's voice had a kind of sneer to it.

"Because I'm too old." Scott suddenly felt ready to explode. "Hey, you want to finish our fight right now? I'm ready, any time you are, and it sounds like you're spoiling for something."

"What about you?" Brad said. "Sounds like you got up on the wrong side of bed this morning and you're trying to blame me for it."

Scott stared at Brad. Maybe he was right. He'd been wanting to hit something ever since the accident. Ever since that moment when he had lost control of what was happening at the practice race, and then Bruno, and finally Rusty. How could he get control of his life again? Mr. Wagner's words came back to him. Take charge, he'd said. Take control.

Then Scott had an idea. It was totally far out, but maybe it just might work. He needed one more dog. He knew where one more dog was. Maybe, maybe, that dog was waiting to be asked.

Scott brushed past Brad and hurried inside to make a telephone call. He wasn't quite sure what he was going to say, so he'd just blurt it out, and hope it worked. And maybe, just maybe, they would understand.

Scott moved through his classes at school, listening, but not thinking, so that sometimes he answered questions wrong or didn't answer them at all when the teacher called on him. He heard some of Brad's friends snickering and twice he caught Michelle staring at him, her eyebrows puckered in a question mark.

It was driving him crazy, having to wait like this. The old man wasn't home when Scott called this morning. Gone to Havre for a new sump pump, his wife had said. That meant Scott had to wait all day until he got home after school. Wait for a telephone call that might or might not come. Didn't that old lady know what a hard time he had with waiting?

Finally the day was over. He rode home on the bus with Caroline and Howdy, and they jabbered across him as if he weren't there.

The bus dropped them off at their stop and Scott walked slowly behind Caroline and Howdy as they followed the path to the house. He wished he'd stayed in town with Brad. It wasn't because he wanted to be with Brad at the vet's, although he was concerned about Bruno. Probably he could have goofed around with Michelle until Mr. Hartfield drove in later. No, he suddenly didn't want to be here at the farm, knowing he should continue to run Kaylah and Chinook but not having the heart to do it.

"Look," Caroline called out ahead of him. "There's that strange car again. It was here a few days ago."

"Yeah, I remember," Howdy said. "It's got a bumper sticker about saving the whales. Isn't that funny? There aren't any whales in Montana."

Scott stopped. Saving the whales? That was their car.

He ran ahead, up the circular driveway, around the house to the back door, slammed into the kitchen. "What happened?" he yelled. They wouldn't come here unless something was wrong.

Mom looked at him, her eyes glistening. Oh, Lord, had she been crying? "They'll tell you, Scott."

Slowly, Scott let himself look at the old couple. The man and woman were sitting at the kitchen table, just as they were when they'd come for Rusty on Monday.

"I thought you'd telephone," Scott began. "Did something happen to Rusty and you came out to break the news? Did he run off again?"

The old man stood up and came toward Scott. "Nothing like that, son. The dog is just fine. He's outside. Didn't you see him?"

"Outside?" Scott felt his breath catch in his throat. "You brought him back?"

Mom took his book bag from him. "He's probably with Kaylah and Chinook in the barn," she said. "Or maybe they've gone out to the field to find David. They do that nearly every afternoon."

"You'll let me borrow Rusty then?" Scott said. "Just for the race, the way I asked? He loves to run with the other dogs."

"Even more," the old man said. "Cameron, I mean Rusty, had already decided what he wanted to do. He had told us in his nice, gentle way, that he belonged here now, not in town with a couple of old people. But we weren't sure you wanted him back until we got your phone call, Scott."

"Wanted him?" Scott said unbelieving. "If you only knew how much I missed him."

"And he missed you." The woman stood up carefully, as if something might break. "He's been sitting by the gate in our back yard, just looking south toward the farm ever since we brought him home on Monday. He wouldn't even eat and that's when we knew. Rusty had been waiting for your telephone call."

The old man finished, "Rusty belongs to you now."

"You mean I can keep him?" But Scott knew that's what he meant, and tears stung his eyes with the realization. He charged out of the back door just as Caroline and Howdy were walking in. They jumped back quickly.

"Some people have rotten manners around here," Caroline yelled after him.

Scott kept running, calling, until he saw the three dogs loping, one after the other, along the fence line by the north meadow. They looked up, saw him, and began to run, flat out. A moment later they greeted him in a wild frenzy. Down he went, rolling over and over with dogs under him, over, and around him. They pulled on his jacket and pants, licked his face until everything blurred.

"Rusty," Scott yelled, managing to grab him. "You're home, you're home." He wrestled with the three of them until his hands and face were sticky with fur and dog spit. When they finally lay around him, panting and waiting for more fun, Scott sat up and looked at each one of them in turn. They stared back, watching for a signal.

"I suppose you're wondering why I called this meeting," he said. Then he began to laugh, and the dogs jumped all over him again.

He didn't even see the old couple walk out of the house and get into their car, but he heard the motor belch into life and looked up quickly. Then the car slowly moved toward the long driveway to the hard road.

Scott stood up and ran after them, the dogs trailing behind him. "I want to thank you," he yelled, waving both arms. "I want to say thank you, forever."

Finally, he stopped running and stood there waving until they drove down the hard road, out of sight.

Later that afternoon he put the dogs together in harness,

and they drove out to the north meadow. They snow had a good crust on it, despite the sunny day, making them cruise right along. Rusty did well, which didn't surprise Scott. After all, he'd run with the other dogs since Scott had started their conditioning and gone to the last race. The dog knew what was going on.

Some time later Scott and the dogs crested the rise of the hill, and he stopped so they could all rest. At the edge of the horizon, the low-lying range of mountains Brad called the Bear Paws stood out as if cut from cardboard.

How far was it to that pass where Brad had gone with his mom? It would be a good place to run the dogs for more serious training, Scott thought.

He felt like singing all the way back to the barn, except he couldn't carry a tune even if he changed his name to Bruce Springsteen. "I'll just have to sing inside myself," Scott told them when they were inside the barn. "This was a great start, more than I hoped for, but we've got to do better. Think we can do it?" He hugged each of them hard before he went in to supper.

Snow surprised Scott during the week. Sometimes it rushed ahead of a stark wind, eager to pile up against fenceposts and telephone poles. Other times it floated lazily into drifts that looked like seven-minute icing covering the pasture.

Scott ran the dogs every day after school and got two long runs in on the weekend. He watched their diet, checked their paws, mended the equipment. When Bruno came home from the vet's on Thursday, Scott felt as if it were a good-luck omen.

"Tomorrow's the big day," Mr. Hartfield said on Friday night at supper. "We'll have to leave before daybreak, so I think we ought to hit the hay early tonight. No TV, okay?"

"Who's going to stay home and take care of Bruno?" Howdy asked, helping himself to more tuna casserole.

Everyone looked at Brad. "He's going with us," Brad said.

"Why?" Mr. Hartfield asked. "He's been so sick, he needs to stay home and rest."

"But I want to go to the meet," Brad said. "So does everyone else. Since Bruno shouldn't stay alone, we'll just take him. Besides, it's not like he's going to do anything. He can sleep in the car instead of the barn."

Brad glanced at Scott, but only for a second. Scott knew why Brad wanted Bruno to go with them. His mom must have written and said it was okay to bring the dog.

"I can take over your job for this one race, Brad," Mr. Hartfield said .

"Or me," Howdy broke in. "Let me, Dad."

"It isn't the dumb job," Brad said. "I just want to be there."

"No." Mr. Hartfield looked at the slice of tomato he was about to eat. "No, we'll be too crowded with four dogs in the car."

"We did it before," Howdy said. He spilled a slippery noodle on his shirt, picked it off with his fingers, and stuck it in his mouth.

"We can stuff Howdy in the back with the rest of the dogs," Brad said. "Since he eats like one."

"I think it's nice that Brad wants to go along for whatever reason," Mom said. "We'll manage, David." She looked at him, sending some kind of message that seemed to signal the end of it.

Except Scott knew it wasn't. Scott knew that Brad planned to stay in Billings with Bruno. Coming home, there would be one less dog and one less kid. There'd be lots of room in the car after the race tomorrow.

•14•

A Race At Last

Everything happened so quickly the next day. It was as if Scott's life was rolling on fast-forward on a VCR. He sat in the back of the station wagon with the dogs, wondering suddenly how he arrived so quickly in Billings. It seemed only seconds ago that they turned south on Highway 87 out of Roundup. Now they were on a main street in town, slowing to look at street signs.

"The fairgrounds is just off Rosecrans Drive," Mr. Hartfield called to him from the front seat.

Scott nodded. The race would begin at the fairgrounds, according to the printout he'd received from Amos. Around the track, then out on the trail that wound south, along the Yellowstone River, and into the meadows before it doubled back and ended at the fairgrounds again. The winner would get a big welcome from the folks in the grandstand, the printout said.

Wonder what everyone else gets, Scott thought. He hoped there would be someone left in the grandstands by the time he came in. No, he couldn't think like that. No negative vibes today. Just good ones, like where will I put the first-place trophy? He grinned as he got out of the car a few minutes later and began to unload the dogs.

Brad helped Scott fasten the excited dogs to their stake-out chains before he said, "I think I'll just walk around and see if I know anyone. You know."

"What are you going to do if there is? Just leave without saying anything to your dad?"

"No, I'll come back and say I'm leaving. And get Bruno." Brad's dark eyes looked worried—deep, dark pools of worry. Today, for the first time, he didn't look as if he wanted to hit somebody. Today, he looked as if somebody could reach out and hurt him.

"But didn't you make arrangements where you were going to meet her?" Scott knew he would have done that much. "Did she say what time she'd get here?"

"No, not . . . not exactly." Brad started to back away.

Suddenly Scott was suspicious. "Then what did she say?" Now he was walking forward as Brad was walking backward. They must look kind of funny to anyone watching, Scott thought.

"Mom never was one to make plans with lots of details," Brad said. "She always said she liked to leave the details to others."

"Come on, Brad, I'm not buying that."

"I'll be back before I leave." Then Brad turned and ran, disappearing into the milling groups of people and dogs.

"Where did Brad go?" Howdy asked when Scott returned to their station wagon and dogs.

Scott began to prepare the sled for the race. "I don't know and I don't care." But the surprising thing was, he did care. He knew that Brad was afraid. He could recognize that in him, now that he'd recognized it in himself. He knew how the guy was feeling and Scott remembered. It didn't feel good to be scared all the time, not even part of the time.

"I'll be your second man," Howdy said. He began to lay out the blue nylon harnesses.

"Good for you, kid." Scott gave him a playful poke in the ribs. "Maybe you can have the job permanently."

"I'll tell Brad he's fired as soon as he comes back." Howdy cupped his hands to his mouth and blew warmth onto them.

Brad hadn't returned when the time arrived to move the dogs to the starting line, so Mr. Hartfield helped instead. It took their combined strength to keep the eager dogs from bolting.

Finally Mr. Hartfield had a chance to ask what Scott knew was on his mind. "Do you know where Brad is?"

Scott looked at him, wanting to say what he knew. Right there, on the tip of his tongue, all his words were ready to jump off into space between him and Mr. Hartfield. He wanted to say, your kid is out there looking for his mom, and scared she won't be there for him, the way he thinks you haven't been lately. I know how he feels because I felt that way for a while about my folks.

But Scott left the words unspoken, left the words inside his head instead of pushing them out where they'd do some good. Suddenly the time for saying them was gone. He pulled his knit cap over his ears and adjusted his goggles.

"It's a go," the starter shouted and the dogs leaped ahead. Scott ran with them, pumping as he held onto the sled, letting them go quickly. Now he gained control of the sled and dogs, slowed them from their killing pace, and they soon began to trot in an easy rhythm. Kaylah cut a straight path the way a good lead dog should.

Finally, Scott dared to jump on the runners as they left the track and moved out of the confines of the grandstand.

Here, the wind found him, cut past his face in knifelike slices and slid down his throat like one long icicle. His eyelashes felt like frozen spikes on his cheeks. Carefully he fit his movements to the sled as if dogs and runners were a part of him.

"Go, dogs, go," Scott shouted. He was high on the feeling of the race, high on running. The sled creaked and whirred over the snow.

Rusty trotted well, keeping up with Chinook and Kaylah without any strain. The dogs were a team, keeping their lines taut against the sled. Their time was not spectacular, but it was a good beginning. Teams needed time to learn about each other; it didn't happen in just one meet. Chinook and Kaylah had the instinct—they were part of the same family right from the beginning. Rusty was like a stepchild, with two families loving him but having to decide which family to live with. And Bruno had only one family to start out with, then got another one in the bargain. Dogs . . . kids . . . we're a lot alike, Scott thought, smiling.

The trail wound sharply to the left now, then followed the river, frozen solid in its banks. Scott heard a sled behind him, its dogs yapping at his.

"On, bye," the driver called and Scott moved over, to give him room. The team, a beautifully matched trio of Siberians, moved quickly ahead.

"That's okay," Scott called softly, as they watched the sled move out of sight through some bare-branched trees. "Just wait till this time next year. They'll eat our snow."

Scott picked up the pace slightly, and the dogs responded. He watched their stride quicken, felt their eagerness through the reins. They ran on in the bright sunshine, and Scott felt great, even though he knew he'd never catch the guy who'd just passed him.

Two more teams passed him before he reached the finish line. Yet it didn't matter. Scott knew his team had done its best and that was good enough for him. It was a great beginning and he'd proved something. He could enter a race and he could finish it.

Mom stood near the finish line snapping pictures as he slowed the team. Then he stopped at one side of the path to give them a quick checkup. The dogs' paws looked all right, no cuts or bruises, but maybe for the longer races, he'd get some leather booties. Maybe Michelle would help him cut and sew them.

"I've got their buckets of water all ready," Howdy shouted as he ran to them. Now he grabbed Kaylah's harness and led the team back to the station wagon, where their stake-out chains were fastened.

"Where's Brad?" Scott asked. "Didn't he come back to help you?"

"No, haven't seen him." Howdy was all business now as he led Kaylah to his can of water.

Scott looked at Mom and Caroline. Mom shook her head and Caroline shrugged. "Maybe he ran away," Caroline said.

"Don't say that." Scott spoke sharply to her.

"Scott," Mom said, "is there something we should know about Brad?"

Scott looked at her, then glanced away. She could always tell when he was lying. And then he breathed deeply. There was Brad, walking slowly toward them, hands deep in his jacket pockets. He shook his head only slightly at Scott, before he opened the car door and slid inside.

"There he is, Mom." Scott pulled off his cap and brushed his damp hair off his forehead.

Mom glanced at Brad in the car, then said, "Let's pack up quickly. I think we ought to start home right away."

So did Scott. Something had happened to Brad. Maybe his mom had said no, he couldn't come and live with her. Or worse, maybe nothing happened. Maybe she hadn't even shown up. From the look on Brad's face, it had to be the worst thing of all.

Mr. Hartfield and Howdy started talking the minute the car pulled out of the fairgrounds. "I've got a great idea, Dad," Howdy said. "Let's get another sled so that next year I can start racing in the one-dog events. Bruno ought to be okay by then."

"Sounds good, Howdy." Mr. Hartfield looked at him in the rear view mirror. "What do you think, Scott?"

"He's Brad's dog. Why don't you ask him?"

"Oh, sure, I planned on it. What do you say, Brad?"

"I think Brad is asleep." Caroline said. She gave him a poke. "Are you asleep, Brad?"

"Not now," he muttered.

"And here's another idea." Mr. Hartfield was really rolling. "We could look around and find another Mal and have a five-dog team. After all, you're not going to get any smaller, Scott. You'll need a larger team in a year or two. Amos pointed that out to me. Said you were pretty big already for a twelve-year-old and showed a lot of strength. You could field a bigger team soon."

"Hey, what about me?" Howdy shouted. "All you ever talk about is Scott."

Mr. Hartfield got the message. "This does include you, Howdy, and Brad and Caroline, too."

"Then say so." Howdy's eyes were flaming.

Scott wanted to laugh. Howdy was so up front you always knew exactly what was on his mind. Scott leaned against Kaylah's thick body the rest of the way home, thinking about Brad, and wondering what had happened, wondering if he'd ever know. Right now, Brad didn't look as if he'd ever tell anybody anything.

Everyone ate a quick supper and turned in early, Brad the earliest of all. Tomorrow, maybe, he'd talk to Scott and Scott would tell him to talk to his dad. Yes, he'd tell Brad that, first thing in the morning. It was time Mr. Hartfield knew how Brad felt about things, especially about his mom and where he wanted to live.

Scott awoke to the smell of pancakes and bacon frying downstairs in the kitchen. It was Sunday morning and Mr. Hartfield was doing his thing, Scott thought. Tradition, he called it. Traditions are a part of every family's life. Got to have them so you'll keep the good ones and then start some of your own. That's what Dad used to say, and now that's what Mr. Hartfield was doing.

Wait a minute here, Scott thought. I've never thought about them together, in one sentence like that before. Never figured that they were alike enough to be in one thought. But they are. Dad and David are a lot alike and it doesn't bother me at all. There, I called him David in my mind. That doesn't bother me either.

He dressed and hurried downstairs to the kitchen. Mom was sitting at the table with Caroline and Howdy.

"Morning, sleepyhead." Mom smiled. "I was beginning to think you and Brad would never get up."

Scott looked around. "Is he still sleeping then?"

Mr. Hartfield turned from the stove. "Must be. Haven't

seen him. This stack has your name on it, Scott." He came to the table balancing three pancakes on a spatula.

"Better save them for Brad," Scott said. "I ought to feed my dogs first."

"Good idea." Mr. Hartfield nodded. "Run upstairs and get him, will you, Howdy?"

Scott grabbed his jacket from a peg by the door. "I'll be back in a couple of minutes." Outside, he stretched on the porch, arched his back, circled his shoulders, and shook himself, the way he'd seen the dogs do it. Then he hurried into the barn and down the aisle to the dogs' stall. The cow and two quarter horses stuck their noses out for a rub as he passed.

Amazing, he thought. We've already turned that into a tradition since I got here. Rub a dub, dub. Four noses to rub.

He let the dogs out and began to mix their food, then he stopped. Four noses, but he'd only rubbed three. He dropped the bag of kibble and ran back to Georgia's stall.

"Georgia," he yelled. He opened the gate and looked into the empty stall, into each corner, as if she could be hiding under a piece of straw.

Then he heard his name being called. It was Mom, calling him back to the house. He knew what she was going to say, what Mr. Hartfield was going to ask. Do you know where Brad is? And, of course, he knew. He knew, all right.

·15·

To the Mountains

"Brad's not in his room," Mr. Hartfield said the moment Scott walked into the kitchen.

"And Georgia's not in her stall," he answered. "Brad's gone, on account of his mom."

"His mother?" Mr. Hartfield looked as if someone had hit him. "How? Where? I don't understand."

Scott shrugged. "He's been writing to her since I came and he thought he was going to meet her yesterday in Billings."

"Billings?" Mr. Hartfield sounded like an echo. "Why?"

"Isn't that where she lives?" Now Scott looked at the faces around him. Caroline and Howdy were standing close together, their fingers touching. Mom leaned against the counter by the sink, shaking her head as if she couldn't believe what she was hearing.

"Brad and Howdy's mother hasn't lived in Billings for over a year. No one seems to know where she's moved." Mr. Hartfield said.

"Where did Brad get her address then?" Scott asked. He glanced out the window. The sky was dirty looking, like erasure smudges on an exam paper. He had seen that look before and knew what it meant.

"She wrote once after she left. Maybe Brad got it then."

Mr. Hartfield suddenly stared at Howdy. "Do you know anything about this?"

"No." Howdy moved closer to Caroline. "No, Brad didn't say anything to me."

"Where do you send her alimony checks?" Mom asked quietly.

"To her lawyer, because that's the way she wanted it." Mr. Bradley walked to the window and stared out of it while everyone watched and waited. "I should have paid more attention to Brad after she left," he said at last. "They were so close." Suddenly he swung around. "Tell me everything you know, Scott."

So Scott filled him in, the words coming in a rush, knowing that he had to go after Brad quickly now, before it was too late.

The quick glance outside told him he had to move fast. Being out with dogs in all kinds of weather told him how to read signs that a storm was piling up, ready to explode, where it was least expected. Maybe the signs had been there when Brad started out this morning, but Scott doubted it.

"I should have seen he was troubled," Mom said. "When he kept looking for mail and not getting it." She looked at each of them. "All those letters he wrote, what happened to them? Did they come back?"

"Don't know." Scott glanced at the back door, feeling its pull, urging him to move before the storm did. "He never talked to me about that."

"I'm sure his mother has a forwarding address we don't know about." Mr. Hartfield shook his head. "She moved around a lot after the separation. She seemed so restless, even before she left."

Scott couldn't wait. The words burst from him. "There's an old cabin Brad told me about. He went there once with her, his mom. I think he's gone there again."

"Why?" Mom was crying now. "Why would he go there? Why didn't he come to one of us? Maybe, if I'd talked to him more . . ."

"Because . . ." Scott stopped. No, he wouldn't say it, didn't have a right. Brad had chosen him to talk to, no one else. Scott knew that the day Brad had found the cabin was the only time he'd felt loved, needed by his mom. Now he'd gone back to find that same feeling again. Only it wasn't there, it was here, here in this house for him and the rest of the family as well.

Scott had to find him, tell him.

"You mean Brad went over the pass?" Mr. Hartfield was staring at him. "Oh, no. I figured he'd just gone to the neighbors. Let me think, I've got to figure . . ."

"I'll go." Scott's hands were on the doorknob now. He risked another glance out the window. The clouds looked like heavy, dense smoke.

Mr. Hartfield began to pace. "I'd better drive over to the Weavers and borrow their snowmobile. Anything else would be too slow." He grabbed his jacket from a peg by the back door. He stopped just before he opened it.

"Why didn't Brad come to me and talk?" Mr. Hartfield asked, looking directly at Scott. "We always talked before."

"You'll have to ask him," Scott answered.

"I'll be back soon," Mr. Hartfield said. "Then we'll all sit down and talk together."

Scott waited until he heard the station wagon rev into action before he opened the back door.

"Where are you going?" Mom hurried toward him.

"Mr. Hartfield doesn't know how fast the dogs can run," Scott said, zipping up his jacket and pulling on mittens. "By the time he gets back from the Weavers, I should be up there." Got to, he thought. Got to keep Brad alive until Mr. Hartfield comes with the snowmobile, to bring him back down the mountain.

Scott stepped outside, felt a hovering stillness that he knew masked the storm's approach. Then he was running across the barnyard and into the barn. He harnessed the eager dogs, keeping their energy barely under control as they leaped and jumped and tugged, knowing what the harnesses meant.

Putting the harnesses on the dogs was the easy part, without help, attaching them to the sled would be a free-for-all. But he'd have to manage somehow. At least the steel-claw brake would help in steadying the sled, keep the dogs from running away.

The dogs ran ahead of him outdoors to the sled where Howdy stood, waiting. "Figured you might need me," he said, grabbing Kaylah's harness.

Scott smiled his thanks. Without any words, Howdy and Scott began to straighten the lines and harnesses. First, however, Scott stamped the brake securely into the ground.

Bruno wobbled around the other dogs, whining as Scott and Howdy worked. "You can't go, Bruno," Scott said. "You have to stay here."

"I'll put him in the barn," Howdy said.

Scott fastened the nylon dog bag to the sled handle, not that he expected to use it, but it was better to be safe than sorry. Then he ran back into the barn and grabbed a thick, old horse blanket for extra security. He didn't expect to use it either, but this trip had a lot of unknowns in it.

"Let me go with you, Scott," Howdy said.

"Can't, Howdy. Next time." Scott pulled on a nylon hood and set his goggles in place.

"Ready?" he asked. Kaylah turned to look at him, waiting for his signal. Now Rusty looked and Chinook, too. They knew today was different.

Scott released the brake and pushed. "Go, dogs, go." The sled leaped forward, moving toward the high north meadow. A little while later they crested the rise and Scott paused, to look below. Behind them lay the house and barn, snuggled warm and invitingly into a cluster of cottonwoods.

And Bruno. Bruno struggled silently after them, and Scott knew he had to take him, too. He secured the sled with the brake, commanded the dogs to lie down, and ran back to get Bruno, wondering if Howdy had deliberately released him. No matter, now. Nothing mattered but to reach Brad in time.

Scott picked up Bruno and staggered back to the sled with him, then quickly zipped him into the dog bag and tucked the blanket around him.

Now Scott stared ahead of them to a cold, white quilting of snow covering the winter rye. Zigzagging across it was a dark path, fresh with recent prints. Brad hadn't been gone long, but it still could be too late. He had to hurry.

"Go," he shouted, and the sled leaped forward again. The storm hit and swirled around them as they cleared the hedgerow and entered the open field. They were fully exposed now, and the wind pushed and pulled, tearing

Scott's eyes, working its way under his collar and fingering his back. He pulled his mitten cuffs over his jacket sleeves while he ran beside the sled to give the dogs a break from carrying his weight. Now he locked his jacket zipper all the way up under his chin. Bruno cozied further into his bag so that only his nose and eyes were exposed.

It grew colder as they climbed. Scott drove the dogs on and on as the whiteness of the world around him numbed his sense of time. The path grew crustier and icier too, so that the dogs stayed on top of it, but their footing lost its sureness. Now intuition took over, guiding Kaylah along the dark path that Brad had left behind.

Finally they needed to stop and rest. Scott called a halt and stepped on the brake, then flopped on the snow beside the panting dogs. He said nothing, he barely had breath for breathing. After a while he wiped his nose and smiled stiffly as he remembered Jamie's description of weather like this. It's a day, Jamie used to say, cold enough to freeze snot.

At last Scott could think about the course again, and he looked ahead to the mountains only to find he was within them. The pass had crested here, onto a small plateau. Conifers, carved by the wind, bowed like soldiers passing in review. Beneath them, a frozen creek lay in broken pieces.

The creek. Hadn't Brad said something about the cabin being near the creek? The thought squirmed in Scott's mind.

"Let's go," Scott yelled. The dogs heard his urgency and jumped to their feet again. Soon they were running hard beside the creek bed as Scott waited for the first sight of the cabin.

Then he saw it, weather-worn and dull gray against the snow. It was so old and broken down, it hardly deserved a name. Cabin meant warm fireplace, soup bubbling on the stove, lights twinkling in the windows. This one didn't have a window, just a hole where once there had been one.

"Whoa," Scott called, and the dogs fell gratefully on the snow. He wondered about Georgia O'Keefe as he walked up to the cabin. Her tracks led here, then disappeared. And Brad? Where was he?

Scott forced himself to look through the hole that once had been a window. He wanted to close his eyes, not look at all, for fear of what he might find. But he had to. Pulling in a breath of air so cold that it pierced the ball of fear stuck in his throat, he peered inside.

Georgia O'Keefe stood on three legs, resting the fourth. Nearby, Brad was rolled into himself on the dirt floor. He seemed to be asleep, at least his eyes were closed. He was so still, so still that . . . oh, God . . .

"Brad," Scott screamed and leaped through the hole.

Georgia jumped but Brad didn't move.

"Brad," Scott yelled again, shaking him. "Brad."

"No." It was hardly a sound. "So cold. So cold. No."

"Brad, you've got to get up. You can't . . ."

"Storm," he whispered. "Never saw it coming. How . . ."

Scott sighed with a great whooshing sound. He's alive, but just barely. Another fifteen minutes and nothing will help. It's that hypothermia Dad used to talk about. Be careful of getting cold and sleepy on the trail.

"Brad, you've got to try." Scott shook him harder, but Brad only lay in a passive, sodden lump. Something else. He had to try something else. But what? Nice wasn't working, maybe he had to be less than nice. How about ornery?

"Come on, peabrain. On your feet. Let's finish our fight." He kicked Brad hard so he'd react. Nothing. Brad sank further into his dirty, damp jacket. His knit cap was soaked and Scott pulled it off, then his wet mittens too. He'd caught the full force of the storm, exposed on Georgia's back.

Scott sat down, rubbed Brad's stiff shoulders, wishing he could think of something more to do. Suddenly all his fear and anger and frustration boiled over at the same instant. He felt like a kettle about to explode. "Brad, you can't die. I won't let you." No more dying around me, he thought. No more.

The impact of his thoughts hit him then. Finally he could love everyone and it was okay. He could love David and Howdy and Brad, yet keep on loving Dad's memory, too. There was room. Even room left over for friends— Jamie, Michelle, and more to come.

He wanted to hit and hug Brad all at the same time. Criminy, wasn't that a weird one?

Warmth, that's what Brad needed now, or he'd die. Scott looked up, Georgia stared down at him. He didn't know anything about horses, how to make her get down on the ground, use her body to keep Brad warm.

But he did know something about dogs. Oh, Lord, love the dogs. The wonderful, wonderful dogs.

Scott scrambled to his feet, ran outside, and unfastened their harnesses from the towline. "Stay, you bozos," he yelled. "I've got another job for you."

Then he unzipped Bruno from his nylon bag. "Come," he ordered and they followed. Kaylah, Chinook, and Rusty leaped through the opening after Scott. He had to lift Bruno through.

"Look who's here, guys. Look who's here."

Brad's dog hobbled over to him, yelping and wagging his tail furiously at the same time. He began to lick Brad's face over and over, smearing it with loving licks.

"Come on, the rest of you. Cuddle in around here." The other dogs sniffed Brad, then settled down close to him. Scott urged and pushed them closer until Brad was surrounded, even covered in places by Mally blankets. Soon the only sound in the cabin was the panting of four dogs. Their warm, earthy breath hovered over Brad.

A moment later Brad murmured, "Umm, feels good, smells bad." A smile appeared on his white, pinched face.

A couple of minutes later he said. "I had . . . to come up here . . . because . . .

Scott interrupted. "Hey, don't talk. Save it for later. Anyway, I understand."

Brad opened his eyes and stared at Scott. "Yeah, I guess you do. Thanks for coming, man."

"No sweat." Scott shrugged, but it was all he could do to keep from crying.

From far away they heard the steady hum of a snowmobile motor grinding up the mountain. It grew steadily closer and would be here in another ten minutes now.

"Listen," Brad whispered. "Is it . . . ?"

"Yeah." Scott hesitated for a second before he finished. "It's Dad."

Then Scott sighed and sat back against the boards of the cabin wall, ready for the moment they could go back down the mountain to home, where the rest of the family was waiting.